SEASIDE SPECIAL:
POSTCARDS FROM THE EDGE

SEASIDE SPECIAL: POSTCARDS FROM THE EDGE

Bluemoose

Copyright © individual authors 2018

First published in 2018 by
Bluemoose Books Ltd
25 Sackville Street
Hebden Bridge
West Yorkshire
HX7 7DJ

www.bluemoosebooks.com

British Library Cataloguing-in-Publication data
A catalogue record for this book is available from the British Library

Paperback ISBN 978-1-910422-42-7

Printed and bound in the UK by Short Run Press

Contents

INTRODUCTION
by Jenn Ashworth   1

THE GULL GODS
by Louise Ayre   5

THE KEEPER OF BOOKS
by Pete Kalu   13

DESTROYING ANGEL
by Paul Kingsnorth   29

THE HUSBAND AND THE WIFE GO TO THE SEASIDE
by Melissa Wan   39

A KINDER LIGHT
by Bethan Ellis   57

TWO WAKES
by Kirsty Logan   73

MONO NO AWARE
by Lucy Wilkinson Yates   85

BLACKPOOL LIGHTS
by Anita Sethi   91

KATY
by Andrew Michael Hurley   97

STILL WATER AND STARS
by Carys Bray   111

CONTRIBUTORS   123

Introduction

Jenn Ashworth

To write about the North West coast is to do battle with the tenacity of stereotype. It is to dodge well-worn evocations of depressed, down-at-heel seaside towns, gaudy sea-front arcades, Ferris wheels, roller coasters and caravan parks and of past-their-best Lakeland towns with stunning views and grim prospects. To write about these places is to somehow acknowledge a variety of well-publicised truths about the social and economic struggles of neglected and disenfranchised populations and also to dig deeper – to find the views and perspectives that surprise and make strange.

No collection, even one including writers as varied and accomplished as the ones you'll meet in this anthology, could claim to provide a complete, exhaustive account of a region which encompasses hundreds of miles of coastline with centuries of complex history, a myriad of urban and natural habitats, and the entire available spectrum of human experience. Under these grey skies and rain-spotted sands lurk a teeming hidden myriad of secret wildlife. Yet the stories included in Seaside Special succeed in gifting us readers with 'postcards from the edge.' These ten writers, some of them established and some being published here for the first time, answer the challenge to 'surprise and make strange' in an array of startling, often discomforting and most of all vivid glimpses of some of the lives and landscapes contained in this stretch of coast.

Proceeding then, in a kind of roughly southwards-heading literary road trip from Solway down to Southport, here are the stories.

Louise Ayre, in 'The Gull Gods' presents the land's edge not as a place of holiday and leisure, but as one of work: her narrator's job is to control (cull) the seagulls along the Solway. The view here is grim and unglamorous: this is no tourist's eye view of natural beauty and breathtaking scenery – even the grace of the birds is only mistaken for beauty and Ayres' Solway is the backdrop for a story of unflinching honesty, determination and even hard-won hope.

Pete Kalu's masterpiece of a story takes an unflinching look at the blood-soaked history of Whitehaven through the lens of a dying plantation owner, returned to 'the wholesome, agreeable atmosphere' of this prosperous Lakeland town. 'The Keeper of the Books' is about reckoning – a final word on the part of a vengeful father blind to the degree of his own sin, perhaps, but also the reckoning made by his silent scribe, Morena. The story is a tussle for control between these narrators, between the slaver and the enslaved, and between perspectives on this picturesque but ultimately culpable town, offered to the reader as the 'last sweet grape of the vine of the West Coast of England.'

The slippery, unbiddable sands around the northern edge of Morecambe Bay are evoked by Paul Kingsnorth's uncanny tale of grief, remembrance and religion in 'Destroying Angel'. There's a flavour of the northern gothic to this tale of loss, spiritual history and the slow motion of ancient landscapes.

Set only a tiny nudge southwards, Melissa Wan's 'The Husband and The Wife Go to The Seaside' narrates a strange holiday in Arnside, where it isn't immediately clear if the haunting that takes place belongs to the landscape itself – the creepy inevitability of the tidal bore links Wan's and Kingsnorth's stories, as well as a tone of human helplessness in the face of darker, more mysterious processes – or to a marriage inexorably going awry.

Bethan Ellis' story 'A Kinder Light' is narrated by one of the anonymous workers on casual contracts whose invisible but necessary labour keep entire towns afloat. This narrator has a past, a life before arrival – but this is elided and instead we are given the story of a quiet friendship, of intimacy at arms-length and the lost edges of a washed-up life. The 'light' in question is not only the sunrise on the wide long curve of Morecambe's seaward edge, but also the gentleness of fragile community, made possible by stories untold and truths unshared.

Some of the stories in this collection engage with stereotypes of seaside entertainments and subtly, with artistry and surprise, move beyond them. I could have filled the entire book with stories about Blackpool, a town that obviously loomed large in the imagination of the writers that submitted to me. Sadly, I was able only to choose three.

Andrew Michael Hurley's short story, 'Katy', presents the reader with a Blackpool we are familiar with: the bright lights of the pleasure beach, the illuminations, the amusement arcades. This is the Blackpool we all think we know – a place of grubby pleasures and easy entertainments, redolent with the smell of candyfloss and fish and chips. But he makes it new – he makes it strange, by giving us the whole place, slot-machines and all, through the eyes of a father desperately searching for his teenage daughter. The possibility of danger is brought sharply into focus. Only towards the close of the story does Hurley allow us to wonder if this father's reunion with his errant daughter is really in her best interests.

In the same territory, Anita Sethi gives us Blackpool through the eyes of a child in 'Blackpool Lights.' For this narrator, Blackpool is a treat of a place, the site of days out, the place where happy memories are made. All this, yes, but also 'the nearest world's edge we have' and the place where the fractures running through a family and a childhood are finally brought into consciousness, acknowledged by the young narrator, but not yet fully understood.

For Lucy Wilkinson Yates in 'Mono No Aware', the town is a place of memory – of lost time, and lost relationships, only glimpsed from afar. "It used to be a classy place," the mother in the story says. Yates' tale – as the best short fictions tend to do – contains lives and worlds within its brevity, with links to Japan and America. The short story, like Blackpool itself, exists on the edge of things, and is knotted into wider narratives that carry the reader across the world and through time.

The Scottish writer Kirsty Logan reminds us, in her story 'Two Wakes', that the North West coast has a long history of welcoming visitors from Scotland during the factory 'wakes weeks' and engages with this annual return through a series of two linked tales set in Cleveleys. Through a delicate, elliptical narrative style, she evokes not only the place itself, a holiday destination of understated and sedate charms, but also that sense of memory, of return, of the looming presence of the past – of what 'going back' might mean for these narrators reckoning with time and with loss.

Moving downwards along the coast, Carys Bray explores the dunes and sandscapes of her hometown, Southport. 'Still Water and Stars' looks both inwards and outwards – at the defamiliarisation of home in the aftermath of a house move, and the loneliness at the centre of a long marriage, suddenly brought into focus by a fresh look at the strange and secret life of the dunes; singing toads and wildflowers.

In *Seaside Special*, then, I endeavoured to curate a collection of short tales that, as a postcard does, presents us glimpses of a landscape. This region is not one that we who live here possess, but one that we who write about are *possessed by*, that is at once known and unknown, familiar and strange, a place of both leisure and work, refuge and threat.

JA
Lancaster – 2018

4

The Gull Gods

By Louise Ayre

It's their wings that always get my attention, out-spreading, white, and salt-coated. They rise in a flurry darkening the sky like a feathered storm cloud. If you do manage to block out the noise of flapping and make yourself deaf to their calls maybe, in the rose-tinted view of some optimistic vegan type, you could mistake this for beauty. They fly upwards then circle back with that determined brutish curiosity; a sense of entitlement and a gnawing hunger-fuelled need to survive. They hang like over-sized paper mobiles on thick air pockets with sharp constant caws against the howl of damp Solway air.

Somewhere along the way I found a name for what we do that felt more fitting than those official and clinical labels they hand out like badges of honour. Those titles are simply a means of justifying a salary and massaging the ego. You would never catch me using the words 'maintenance' or 'management' to describe what I do. All of it is just a trick of language used to conveniently paper over reality. In my mind of too many films and too few alternatives, we are the 'death-bringers', and no matter their apparent stupidity I am sure the gulls know this.

Gull intelligence has been a regular subject of debate over cups of cheap company tea, the majority opinion usually being they have none. Occasionally there is the tongue-in-cheek suggestion that they've evolved an internal radar of sorts, or even a shark-like sense of smell, it would explain how they seem able to detect a bag of chips within a ten-mile radius. Theories are offered up with bravado shortly before the predictable chorus of 'rats with wings' starts up, a phrase I'm pretty sure is more suited to pigeons. Pigeons really are disease-ridden; they drop their black and white shit on your garden furniture and then on that rare fair weather day you sit outside you'll eat your lunch off that table. I wouldn't.

You've got to respect the gull. The scraggy one-legged pigeon will stalk you for your Maccy D's fries; a gull is much more ballsy. Just you sit at the end of the Whitehaven Sugar Tongue with an open bag of chips and see how many gulls you have to fight off from dive-bombing your lap. I've seen the way they eye the van, there's something there, ticking away.

"They're thick as pig shit," Steve had said between coffee-slurps.

The comment came at the end of a conversation about the new business park – never trust an architect to take pest control into consideration.

"I can't understand why we don't just poison the lot of them," Steve continued, "call it a mass cleanse."

He had been in the job a little over three years, practically a veteran compared to me, and often boasted he knew all the 'control and elimination' methods, the pros and cons of each, plus a few of the niche practices we don't talk about, at least not publicly. John stood next to me and I took a discreet step away, avoiding eye contact.

"That's a bit extreme don't you think?" I said.

Steve looked at me with his mug resting against his protruding lips, but instead of responding took another deep mouthful. I watched the jump of his Adam's apple as he swallowed. The *you're just a soft touch, love* line had grown tired for him too so that now, when he deemed me to be behaving too in line with my sex, he simply chose not to respond.

"Don't be daft Steve," John piped in and I turned my attention to my own now tepid drink, "we do that and half you lot will be out of a job."

We all laughed.

"Just making conversation," he said with a glance my way, "too many birds can really ruin a place."

Weeks later we were all called into the office for an 8 a.m. meeting. Hushed voices told the rumours in hurried whispers. Some of us had already seen the story on the local news read by stone-faced reporters *still awaiting comment from JC Pest Services.*

"We believe it was a home-made recipe," John told us.

His face tightened as he spoke in clipped phrases that washed over me and I was left with only traces of words that stuck to me like rice – *an isolated incident.*

I tried to picture Steve concocting his own special feed. The thought of him donning an apron while stirring up a thick mix of grain and seeds felt comical. Still it was preferable to the alternative, the one I couldn't seem to shake. It was an image of thick rubber gloves and careful measures, the acidic whiff of chemicals, crushed powders, and Steve's steady hand pouring liquid into a measuring jug. I thought of bomb makers.

It had happened at the breaking of dawn. Bird by bird, opened up like crimson flowers in blooms of hot red against falling white feathers. Bird after bird, trying to fly from the small bloodied explosions of their own flock before they too ruptured from the inside out.

Today I'm alone as I watch them. After a few minutes a large male throws his head back into a long call. It's a droning caw, something between laughter and a fire alarm, and the others are quick to join in. They fight between themselves, snapping at one another and spreading wings. I remind myself – I have done this before, it's my job – and by now it's verging on second nature. Still, I have never done it alone and the empty space around me, the new cold void which was previously filled with at least some form of conversation, leaves an unwanted cleft for my thoughts to fill.

Pest control wasn't exactly the job I pictured myself doing. I don't think anybody does. Unless you're Steve, then maybe it's high up on the list of things you might want to do when you grow up. Maybe for him it was between this and pyrotechnics. It would make sense. I, on the other hand, had sat in front of my crumpled careers advisor in what was basically an oversized cupboard while he asked me about my interests. Pest control didn't come up on his list of suggestions, I made that move all on my own.

A teacher, that was what I wanted to be once upon a time. The idea of that now, of standing in front of all those kids and trying to just make them behave like something resembling small humans, never mind impart some actual knowledge, sounds like my idea of a nightmare. At no point has anyone ever turned to me and told me that I'm sensible or responsible and I'm guessing they're the sort of thing that come under the 'essential skills' section for any role involving children, or other humans for that matter. This is apparently less of an issue with animals, especially if those animals happen to be dirty, uninvited and numerous.

I tend to make mistakes, I guess that is one thing that can be said about me. I do it with such frequency that I have even come to recognize the specific glare my mistakes trigger, the one where they – the teacher, the mother, the manager – fix you with a frown and finally exhale a sigh that flares their nostrils. They aren't angry is what they usually say, if they say anything at all, they're *just disappointed*. I know it's not entirely my fault, mistakes seem to gravitate towards me or I manage to stumble onto them. That was what I had been trying to explain this morning.

"I wouldn't send you alone if I didn't think you were capable," John had said.

His words pricked at me. They seemed a little too convenient. Worse still, they sounded scripted. Knowing him, he had probably rehearsed the whole speech that morning. He'd have reassured himself – in front of his bathroom mirror – that I would, of course, be flattered. Capability wasn't what I had meant and he knew it, I had been trying to explain something but lost the thread of it before it dawned on me he wasn't even listening. Sending me alone today was John's ingenious solution to the possibility of gossip between staff following the Steve incident. The unvoiced accusation was that I, just like all the others, was a talk risk. The insult of it made me swallow down any more objections.

I take the climb up the ladders at a slow pace, with one hand pulling up the heavy feed bucket: its handle presses into my palm and my right shoulder is weighed down taut against my neck. There is the familiar putrid smell of sour fish and the feeling of sickness from this morning lingers like a threat. There are no nests here, not yet, but as I step onto the roof I am eyed all the same by its waddling occupants. From here I can see the white crests of the waves and as the wind pushes back my hair it brings with it a fine spray of seawater that clings to my skin.

It's a straggly male that comes closest. One of his wings is bent out of shape but his injury seems only a minor inconvenience to him; if anything, it has piqued his determination. He is the first to feed on the mix of nourishment and chemical. He is greedy and excited. At the noise of the grain the flocks descend from every direction and the sound of wings beating upon the air drowns the rain-like sound of grain hitting the roof. I empty the entire bucket, turning it up to spill even the stubborn grains from the base where they have clung together in small clusters, and watch as the gulls compete for every piece.

Back in the van and with the birds focused on the food the sky feels still, but it will only be a short pause in the usual chaos. This doesn't feel like death, it's something else, a change. I wonder again at what point we, all of us, changed to such a degree that we began to play God.

I cannot forget the waiting inside me, such a small insignificant thing, a parasite. When I'm not thinking about that I'm replaying the conversation from last week, untangling it in the hope of finding some other meaning.

"I can't keep doing this Becky."

John's voice had sounded hollow around the words and I waited for him to look at me, hoping that if he did something in him would change. The words I had practised stuck in my throat.

"I just can't do this to her, not now."

When he looked at me it was in pleading. I didn't want to see that in him but still I felt the urge to step around the desk he had arranged so tactfully between us. His face was drawn down, deepening the creases at his eyes. I wanted to reach out to him; instead I tightened my posture and picked out the right words.

"I know."

"I was going to leave her," he began again, "you know I was, but I just can't be that guy."

There's a photo of them both on his desk, the holiday in Italy, just after she got the all clear. I tried not to look at it for too long but I couldn't turn away from their smiling faces and her short-cropped blonde hair, luminous in the perfect Italian sun. I had been on the verge of stealing that life.

"I don't want you to be, either."

The words were the husk of some truth somewhere, because I don't want him to be that guy but only because I'm not supposed to, I would still accept it. I would still walk away merrily into the sunset with only the briefest of glimpses back at the woman I betrayed.

It had been a short-lived thing, an ill-judged bit of fun, just another silly little mistake. If I can just make myself push down the cold feeling of hurt and panic, I can hold out hope that something bigger than myself will give me an answer. Someone other than me will take control and tell me what I'm supposed to do now. I just wrongly thought John would be that person.

I watch as some of the gulls leave the roof having had their fill. They do not go far but their calls are fewer and quieter. Soon they will build more nests along the slats of this roof but the clutches of speckled eggs they lay will never hatch and this is how we play God now, with this and so many other things because apparently, it's kinder than poison.

Before I turn the ignition, a gull descends onto the bonnet of the van. It doesn't look at me as it pads with its webbed feet across the paintwork but I notice the same bent wing. It stretches it out and after another step spreads both wings and hops to the tarmac. I keep watching as it flies in small bursts. Steve was right, they are not the most intelligent of creatures but they are damn well determined to survive.

I think about the small bomb inside me waiting to explode and I think about crimson upon white feathers. We are all just playing at being Gods.

The Keeper of Books

By Pete Kalu

A curious Vellum document written in real hand, found among assorted deeds within a chest on a Scottish estate. Slightly foxed though this does not affect its legibility. Various annotations and embellishments including pencilled notes. In good condition overall. This is an unsigned and extremely rare original and is exhibited and for sale by auction without guarantees. Any claims as to its provenance whether written or oral and whensoever made, the seller hereby expressly repudiates. Estimate: £80-100

This is the Last Will & Testament of Horton Gideon Bradley, of —————————————————————————— as witnessed this day of our Lord Third October 1765 by his house servant and scribe of this text, Morena, dictated on his deathbed.

Whereas I am at peace with the Lord and have visited Church and commended my soul to my Maker whose forgiveness I have sought for all sins committed and having donated a sum to the maintenance of the church in recompense of my mortal transgressions ....

Water please again, Morena. Where was I?

...therefore, I leave to my son a sixpence, which is in excess of the value of the scoundrel, wastrel, dissolute and reprobate issue of my loins. His prodigious talent for surfeit, bacchanalian excess and licentiousness together with his utter disregard for the legal prohibitions on fronts as varied as public pissing, gambling, miscegenation, fraud and the passing of fraudulent Instruments (many bearing my name), impersonation and degenerate practices against God which he appears to have himself invented not even the Spaniards having devised such abominable couplings; all these sins being such an affront to moral standards as would offend all upstanding members of civil society and clearly render him in this moment unworthy of greater benevolence on my part; furthermore...

The Lord is all forgiving. This father is not. Neither, in due course, permit the miscreant ingrate to be buried anywhere close to me, that when I rest in peace I may rest truly and properly in peace.

More water. It is fine, I shall go on. No, omit nothing, write exactly as I say. We can amend later.

There is a sweetness to the air of Whitehaven which is signature of its wholesome, agreeable atmosphere, it is indeed the last sweet grape of the vine of the West Coast of England. A man may go about his business in this fair town without petty restriction and by an attentive, assiduous manner proceed – with a tug here and there of trusty bootstraps – to amass or augment his fortune. Such a path I have endeavoured to tread in my humble way and have achieved, by the by, some modicum of success thereat.

Morena, the glass of water to my lips again please. You think my praise of that cursed town, Whitehaven sufficient? If not, add more here.

There is of course great beauty to be witnessed in the tranquil and orderly loading and unloading of cargo at the wharves of

Whitehaven: the balletic sweeps of the cranes, the doughty exhortations of the stevedores, the porters' antic scuttling. The trade in sugar in particular has been a benediction to the town, a boon to its coffers and a blessing to its tea shops.

Read your scribbling back. That is fine, let us continue.

Such convivial civic atmosphere and munificence have been in no small way aided by the financial contribution in the form of Duties, Levies & other assorted Taxes of the Estate – an Estate run smoothly and efficiently to the admiration of all.

Come closer and fan my neck, my cheek, Morena, the heat rises insufferably in me. Yet I will go on. Quicken your quill.

It was not always thus. When the call of duty came, I cast aside my literary aspirations – several of my poems had garnered enquiries from reputable London publishers – and set about tending to the family plantation located –––.

We have long had a presence at this colony. Burke's Peerage lists my great grandfather as a Major in the British Army posted to these parts and evidences his courageous and daring exploits while here stationed.

Morena, the Major's achievements are written in the greatest copperplate somewhere among the documents. Copy the wording into this section of the Testament. Numerous Certificates and Awards. Vindicated in two court cases. Two further Murder charges dropped. Set it all down here, that the family honour survive the ruinous deeds of my son, this Testament to become one part of the counterbalance. It is fine. One more sip.

Aside his military sense of organisation and his sterling competence in the matter of the explosive clearing of grounds yet by dint of various unfortunate financial Adventures, the

Major at his demise left the Estate in some considerable disarray hence, with the skip of a generation or two, my summons.

I did my duty by the family. Succeeding generations will find here now an orderly and handsomely regulated estate of some nine thousand acres with hogsheads and puncheons trundling day and night upon its sturdy tracks. The indexes will show an annual healthy accumulation of cane, molasses, muscovado and rum, acres of cacao trees and indigo crops; also seasoned negroes, free of most diseases, utensils, cattle and horses, provision crops, pasture grass, a skilled body of a workforce comprising both negro slaves and white servants. This is my legacy. How was it so ordered in such an invidious landscape?

Morena find the word I need because invidious is not quite it. Water. My lips. Let us return. Adverse? Yes, adverse will do.

In the midst of hurricane, earthquake, pestilence and revolt, determination is not enough. The Keeping of Books is of the utmost importance in this endeavour. Ironic that I began with ambitions as a poet and my legacy is yet contained within Books, simple numbers standing in the place of florid metaphors. You will find at the Estate an accurate and complete Store Book, Boiling House Book, Still House Book, Slave Book, daily Labour Book, Stock book of creatures both horned and others; also trained book-keeping staff and a well grooved method for the upkeep thereof.

Cane is crushed in prodigious quantities thanks to this regimen and while the varying quotas set down in the Laws of Deficiency were never quite attained, yet still the Estate proved sufficiently congenial as a place of work that a staff of one white man to fifty negros was achieved most years without makeweights.

Hic multa desiderantur . . . . .

... so prolific and assiduous was I in my work that I believe the townsfolk at one time named a species of rat after me, an accolade, bizarre though it might seem, I fully embraced, for, like the rat, in those years, I was both ubiquitous and well fed.

Cross out these last two sentences, Morena, they are out of tone. Where was I?

I leave to my son a sixpence, which is in excess of the value of the ingrate, reprobate and dissolute issue of my loins...

I repeat myself?

In contrast to my wayward good-for-nothing offspring about whom I have hereby drawn a line in this Testament, there has been at the colonial Great House in general a sophisticated atmosphere such as would rival the merry balls of London or Paris or fair Whitehaven herself. Far from that mocking myth that we planters are for the most part gross illiterates, there is in these colony environs a deep thirst for knowledge, a fine body of elocutors, philosophers & orators, ostentatious sartorial display in both feminine & masculine forms & an appreciation of the arts as evidenced by the theatrical days, French dances & poetry recital evenings that are sustained here each season, not forgetting the superb pageant upon the completion of the harvest of the season's canes. I have oftentimes thrown open the grounds of the Estate for such divertissements and all visitors have remarked on the delicacy of behaviour at these gatherings and what a valuable jewel to civilization the Estate has become, a comely oasis of order and culture.

It was not always thus. I bear the scars of its transformation not only in my mind but even on my body. Life in the early days of my stewardship was Hobbesian – of a brutishness unrivalled in the annals of planting. It is germane at this juncture that I turn to explain the welts that cross my upper back; there have been many rumours as to their provenance, some scurrilous, others phantasmagorical; it behoves me to set the story down here straight, if not quick: we needs must take a circuitous route in this tale.

.　　　.　　　.　　　.　　　.　　　.　　　.　　　.

Desunt nonnulla　　　.　　　.　　　.　　　.　　　.

.　　　.　　　.　　　.　　　.　　　.　　　.　　　.

More water, Morena. Now read it back. Good. Why did you include that about the slave conditions? Delete. Delete. Delete. Let me check. Give me the water let me scrub it. Good. Tonight copy this all out again without the deleted text.

The Estate operates by a number of ledgers detailing income and outgoings. Among those outgoings is the cost of servicing assorted mortgages accumulated through the years. Wags say that the mark of the grandee is the grandeur of his debts and the Estate debts are indeed grand. Putting to one side the effects of the Major's financial Sallies which make up a moiety of the antique mortgages and which time and negotiation have found me unable to shift, more recent financial instruments I have took up for sounder reasons, be that to buy further land or to invest in new machinery.

After calculation, and with some trepidation at the existing debt magnitude, I purchased a full cartload of slaves at auction,

18

comprising thirty-one fit males, fifteen females and assorted children in visible good health, approximately sixty hands in all. They were seasoned on the Estate and adjusted well with no losses from typhus, eating of soil or the darkness. Upon release from the seasoning cage, the younger among them were inducted as apprentices with the usual duties. As per custom, the fittest among the adult males were assigned to the Number One gang, including a slave I named Frederick, who also went by the name Olu.

The crop that year was looking bounteous and barring Acts of God would yield a handsome profit, compensating for previous, less climactically propitious years.

To gather the crop, I determined that the whole estate should be driven to its fullest extent. I took personal charge, ensuring the Boiling House had no rest: it is fatal economics in these circumstances not to have the mill fed every hour that daylight gives us with cane which in turn means a full effort from all hands in field and Works.

A system so finely calibrated was yet vulnerable to the slightest disruption. When the puncheons and hogsheads failed to accumulate in the manner expected, I investigated. My scrutiny soon revealed the cause of the problem. Cane was being reaped only in fits and starts. The overseers told of a general go-slow of the One gang, symptomatic of burgeoning malcontent, and such sentiment now spreading across other gangs. Seek the main troublemakers, I counselled, and make an example of them such that all others fall quickly in line, for discipline meted quickly and with draconian force is more effective and therefore kinder in the long term than a succession of small corrections: the knotted stick must yield to the cowhide and rope.

I know this account pains you, Morena, yet we must continue. Let the inkwell catch your tears. Drink. Where now? Are you ready?

A messenger rode up at this point with the urgent news that my wretched son was introducing discord once more to the town of his birth. I duly left the plantation post haste for Whitehaven but not before confirming in the overseers their instructions.

Dab my forehead, Morena, let the cloth rest there a while... It is good.

Those several long weeks of the lengthy sea voyage gave me time to consider my son's antics – whether they were the sign of some born infirmity of the mind, whether some vapour he had breathed had disturbed his faculties or whether perchance the excessively constricted clothes he was wont to wear caused insufficient blood to rise to his brain and so atrophied his reason. I knew not what was the cause of his malady but I knew full well what lay in store for me at port. I planned, with the judicious deployment of a large brimmed hat, to avoid detection by the mob.

Fair Whitehaven, a town well named, its purity a matter of renown, its reputation unblemished, a shining emerald in the diadem of English ports. Never does my heart not lift upon sight of its wondrous docks. The breeze that meets the arriving folks on foredeck is a heady admixture of tobacco, sugar and coffee commingled with an exquisite, salty air that stiffens the limbs and enlivens the minds of its doughty townsfolk. My feet fair floated over the harbour cobbles in elation at my return. I huddled low, pulled my hat down over my ears and stepped fast. Alack, in vain was my disguise. Even as rain inevitably follows shine, petitioners trumpeting my son's alleged misdeeds soon fell upon me at quayside; I was accosted on all sides, my hat swept off my head. With difficulty, I shook off my would-be interlocutors and whipped the carriage horses swift to the courthouse, the better to appraise the trail of destruction my ill-begotten fool of a son had wrought.

Judge A– ushered me to the Assize Sessions Chambers and over cognac welcomed my presence and intervention, agreeing regarding my son that for a man of such refined stock to be grouped with the common criminal class by the constabulary was a manifest error that no amount of evidence, even unto the constabularies' own eyes could overthrow; and only a procedural infelicity caused his discomfit in jail to be prolonged.

I wished to move quickly to the despatch of this conversation but Judge A– had something of the pedant in him, and, warmed by the brandy, insisted for the sake of procedure on reading me the arraignments. At length he concluded with an encomium: that one man should have so thoroughly rhymed, sung, drank, fought, whored, slept, sworn, duelled, took snuff, visited plays, bilked coachmen and kicked fiddlers so fully in such a short sojourn is in some perverse way, impressive. I urged the judge to desist. *Your point is made your honour,* I told him.

More water, Morena. Perhaps something a little stiffer, and the cloth dipped in cold water and replaced upon my head.

The cognac despatched, the judge moved to the prescriptive part of his perorations: that I render to him yearly for the next five years five hogsheads of rum in satisfaction of his judicial leniency, such number to be added to the fourteen hogsheads already earmarked in settlement of my son's previous delicts. This induced no little exasperation on my part and I argued strenuously, it being the case, the total yearly was advancing at such a rate these annual barrels would soon approach a score in number. This concern the judge swatted away. He returned to his cups with a small guffaw, indication that our meeting was at its end.

I left the courthouse with a lingering sense that Judge A– enjoyed my son's little sorties, his misadventures perking up his otherwise dull round of petty thefts and little assaults while replenishing his liquor cellars.

Never one to tarry, next I did the rounds of polite society in the requisite sack cloth and ashes. A Duchess and Duke who had supplied a credit line against a false instrument; an ancient Madam of grand assets persuaded she was finally about to marry; a Portuguese Countess turned investor in non-existent tobacco crops. There were manifold others, all irate for diverse reasons. In the course of their complaints I heard sufficient homilies to compose my own Book that could rival that of Lucretius: *Nemo fit repente turpissimus.* Beware the Lethargy of Sin and Impenitency. Shame is the great Bridle that restrains Human Nature from running into all kind of Wickedness &c &c.

By day's end I had an empty purse, sore lips and a tear-soaked shoulder but had sufficiently repaired with coin what little reputation the family had left that I saw no need to dally any longer amongst the ermine and petticoats. As eventide fell, I paid the surgeon's bills for the knit of my son's bones {right shin and left forearm} then went on to a certain Whitehaven whorehouse to settle his debts therein. I was for some while detained at this locale, surprised as I was by the amount sought in satisfaction, though upon sample I considered it a fair bargain overall especially given the willingness to move surprisingly distant from convention in various matters. Doubly enlightened, and rendered somewhat light-headed by the lingering effects of the whorehouse, I set off to debtor's prison to minister some of the court-gathered homilies to my unworthy son and, should he evince the necessary repentance, to bail him.

I found the blockhead lubricated and far from contrite, indeed boastful in the maximum. He described to me with glee the ups and downs of his fists and breeches, and the gape and swallow of his purse. I admonished him, counselling it is a thing of a most mischievous consequence to ruin and undo honest innocent women, and a double sin to defraud nobility of their estates. I pressed also my incredulity at his conviction that he might, in partaking intercourse with a second harlot, cure the poxes received from a first, it being such a transparently and dismally erroneous calculation that it beggared belief as well as the pocket. All of this was as pissing into the wind; he declared the homilies *Non Gradus Anus Rodentum* and was untrammelled of even a smidgeon of that commodity – shame – so necessary for moral improvement.

It was only several hours later upon my return, that, soberer, and more aware of his continuing imprisoned circumstances, he expressed profuse contrition and in the usual manner promised to compensate me my injuries on his account. I was unpersuaded of the sincerity of his emotions, but I relented, accepting his offer of a return to the plantation though insisting on providing him with a beefy escort to steer him in the shortest, most expedient route to the docks and sea passage onwards.

Of course, the moment he was freed, he absconded, giving his flat-footed escort the slip, and hot-footing to a destination rumoured to be Italy. I was at this point called urgently to return to the plantation and so had no recourse but to let the matter of my Godforsaken son in the interim lie.

More water Morena, and ease my pillows lower. My energies deplete. Bend closer for I have strength if not to talk then to whisper.

I bid sweet Whitehaven farewell, glanced one final time at its glittering waters, its fragrant company, its enchanting docks.

.   .   .   .

Hic multa desiderantur .   .   .   .   .

.   .   .   .

There was gaiety and brisk business at colony port since several ships had arrived with provisions as well as fresh supplies of slaves and incidentals. I pressed through this ruckus and made way to the Estate. I arrived as night fell and found all in disarray.

Slave drums were talking. It meant trouble. Morena, I know you understand those drums. You never told me what they said. Why was that? Now as then you look away. No matter. The drums. The disarray. I had the books brought to me and they quickly showed disorder was pushing the plantation to the brink of financial disaster.

The overseers apprised me of the situation. In brief, they had failed to carry out my instructions with sufficient severity and revolt had fomented among the slaves: several runaways, widespread feigning of sickness and the day to day business of the plantation all but suspended. To cap all this, Agnew, the chief overseer, a dedicated man full of guile and wisdom, had been pulled from his horse and strangled to death. The culprit was that same Frederick mentioned above. After committing this murderous deed he had fled to join the band of runaways in the hills.

I could barely suppress my rage – at the overseers for their incompetence and at the state of affairs this had led to. That very morning as we white men spoke, drums were talking.

> *See how the birds soar from the trees and fly*
> *wherever they wish? Why not us too? I would*
> *rather die a human being than live like a dog.*
> *We outnumber them sixty to one. Even with their*
> *whips and guns, we can overwhelm them. Agnew*
> *was the start, not the finish. Let us end what we*
> *have begun.*

My first order was to silence those drums. All drums were seized and destroyed, and a warning issued – anyone found in possession would be chained to the ground and burned. The hills still echoed with their infernal rhythms but at least no longer did any drums on my plantation talk.

24

Next, I turned my attention to this Frederick. I had brought into the courtyard the woman he had been sleeping with and her two children. They were now my drums, played with whip and cowhide. The bait proved good. By the fourth night, Frederick appeared, unpenitent. No matter, I had him roped, manacled and caged.

There was a sigh of relief among polite society. It is a generally known fact that, once white blood reaches the lips of slaves, a taste is developed, and more is sought.

I digress, Morena, where was I?

I ordered all slaves assembled by the hanging tree. Not the head slave driver, nor the two remaining overseers were willing to strike the necessary blows. It fell to me to administer the punishment.

I had the rope crossed at the slave's wrists then yanked high so only the tips of his toes felt the earth. I commenced with the whip. If he cried out, I heard nothing. I worked the whip with all my force. Though sore of arm, I kept on till all flesh was peeled from his ribs and his lungs were visible. His life about to depart, he somehow managed to call out with his last breath. All heard. It was a phrase in Creole. *Massa, me ah come fuh yuh!* Or some such curse. Of course, the gathered slaves immediately looked upon me as a man condemned, such is their belief in what they call Obeah and we call superstition. I ordered the body be left to hang until the birds had clean pecked it to glistening bone, that all may remember the price of rebellion. I retired to the Great House.

My body sore from my exertion with the whip, the heat high in my sleeping chamber, I was a little downcast at the waste of a prime specimen of a slave, but was nevertheless encouraged by the speed with which work on the plantation had resumed: the vista from my chamber window was once again one of complete normalcy. I lay on my bed and fell to a fitful slumber.

That night I heard singing, Morena, a strange singing. Did you hear that song, or did I dream it? One further curious point, Morena, no bird ever alighted on his corpse, a fact I put down, not to any superstitious matter, but perhaps some biological curiosity. More water to my lips. It is good.

The next morning, I replaced both overseers – cowardly men whom the slaves no longer feared. I had all fit male field slaves from Number One gang sold on, and salt-water slaves bought who were properly submissive. I increased punishments and increased the reward to both field and house slaves who leaked news of impending trouble and identified malcontents. It was a febrile time. I slept with a pistol by my side. Slowly, order was restored, or so it appeared.

This next is surmised, my recollection necessarily blurred by the effects of my drowsiness on the night in question; I will not dwell long here nor cast blame, I simply set it down for the record. I had thought the worst over. Yet somehow on the night in question – that fateful night – a slave, of such dark hue he seemed only a shadow, sneaked into the Great House. With great nimbleness he evaded house slaves and servants, evaded even you, Morena, a seemingly impossible feat so lightly you sleep, but one nevertheless achieved.

The interloper stole into my room and called out some phrase which, slumbering as I was, I could not make out, other than that it was accusatory. He then set upon me with a whip. Befuddled by the stinging pain, I suffered such blows as would have killed a lesser man, but at last my hand found the pistol by my pillow and I fired. The bullet seemed to go straight through him, though I am sure on reflection I simply missed. The intruder fled. Astonished that neither house slave nor servant had roused, not even upon the report of the pistol, I woke the house to give chase. Yet by the time the house mustered, the interloper was long gone.

Blood slew from my back and arms, I felt myself dangerously weak. A doctor by chance passing that night was diverted to my aid and, after compresses and tight bandaging, the blood loss was staunched. My injuries in due course healed, though the scars to this day remain.

I am no fool. I know someone betrayed me that day, someone close. No ghost of Frederick entered my quarters in the Great House but a mortal man; heads had turned away. Even you, Morena, at one point I suspected. For many months afterwards, I was wracked with a Biblical fear – my enemies multiply – yet I did not turn tail and flee the colony as weaker-willed planters might.

Where am I? Afterwards? Yes.

Gossip vaulted. Slaves fanned the fable this assault was the revenge of Frederick; waggish tongues in Spanish Town opinioned it likely a dispute over gambling debts, still others cited the lust for revenge of my son. All these surmises were wrongheaded, and I have hereby set the record straight. I restored order. I quelled rebellion. Our plantation shall prosper now and forever more. Not for nothing did the Major choose as family motto *futui et vici* – I have fought and conquered.

Morena, more water.

I turn to the apportionment of my Assets. I leave to you, Morena, ten pounds current money of Jamaica, an annuity to be paid each year on the day of your birth which happy occasion was the kindest gift the good Lord bestowed on me. When I think of the contrast between your unswerving loyalty and the persistent perfidy of my son, I feel the circumscription of the laws and customs pertaining to inheritance an unjust imposition. Come closer, press your ear full close to my lips, it is meet and well you should know this. You are my daughter, Morena, I imagine you have already guessed. Had your mother survived she would be proud. Bless your soul, no tears, let me go on.

I leave one quarter of my estate, after the settling of debts to my first cousin

.   .   .   .

Hic multa desiderantur .   .   .   .   .

.   .   .   .

I was happiest as a child, Morena, those halcyon days ... Do I drift? Weakness overwhelms me. I fear this text rambles. We shall have to start again tomorrow. Yes, tear it up, Morena, tear it now. The heat ... My brow ... Ah f --

Desunt nonnulla

Destroying Angel

By Paul Kingsnorth

There were four people in the church for morning prayer. Four people, all over sixty. One of them asleep. I always applaud the vicar, at the end. Every church I go to, I applaud the vicar. Sometimes I approach him afterwards and I say, *it's a hard job you have, vicar.* Somebody should tell them, somebody should show some appreciation. *Everyone's a pagan now, vicar,* I say. *Cars, shopping, the internet. No-one believes anything. But it's a test. God has set us a test. You did well today,* that's what I say to him. It's usually a him, though one of the churches I visit has a woman now. I don't know what they're complaining about. The church needs all the help it can get. She's very nice. I say the same to her. *Hardest job in the world you have,* I say to her. She's usually too busy to talk after a service, but she smiles at me. They have a lot to think about.

I go to a service every day if I can. There are many churches around here, of course, scattered around the Bay, in all the old villages. No shops left in most of the villages, pubs closing or turned into fancy restaurants. Big silver cars parked up every pavement, doors closed and bolted. Nobody who lives there was born there. I don't know where these people come from. It doesn't matter now. It is too late now to worry about any of that.

What matters now is not here amongst us, I think.

They're centuries old, some of these churches. Stained glass, roof bosses, Norman doorways, all that. Sometimes folks will come in with booklets looking for reredos or rood screens or historic fonts. If I see them, I tell them: it's the words you should be looking for. You can see an old sixteenth century door anywhere, but a good sermon: a good sermon is a summoning. From across the centuries, from over the waters, the voice moving on the waters, coming closer. Will it come in? Will it choose to come in and settle, just for a moment, amongst us? A good sermon is an incantation. It is ritual magic. These buildings are nothing without the words.

At the beginning of any service the church is empty like a wood in winter. That's how you can tell if a sermon is a good one, if the vicar deserves your applause: if they get the spell right, you will hear the Lord enter the building. You will hear the coming. It makes a sound, gentle, rushing. You will feel the Spirit curl itself around the roof beams and settle in. You will be in the presence.

The Spirit will come if you sing to it. It is an animal that must be gently enticed. If you sing it in to the building with the correct words, it will come. It does not care how many people are waiting.

I do not care about the rood screens.

This is the month that Anya died. November. It is six years now. She did well. We did well. Nobody stays married anymore, like nobody goes to church. But we did. We stayed married because it was our task, it was our work, and because we did our work well we built love from it. These people who think love drops from the sky, or is cheap on some supermarket shelf, that you can return it and ask for a refund. These people who think everything is cheap, or should be. Love is work, like God is work, like anything real is work. Love is a practice. Our practice lasted for twenty-seven years.

When I walk home after a good sermon I have only one foot in this world. On this morning I am talking of, this morning when there were only four people in the church, I was passing through a small wood that stands between the village and the shore of the Bay. There is a kissing gate and a clear path and it was mid-morning in October. There were still leaves on most of the trees. Rooks were gathering above the oaks in flocks, bigger and bigger each day as they spiralled towards winter.

And then there was somebody in the wood with me.

When I entered the wood I was still in the church, still in the presence of the Spirit, still with the prayer. I had brought the words with me. *In his hand are all the corners of the earth, and the strength of the hills also.* I spoke them aloud as I walked, perhaps. I do that sometimes. I wonder if this was what made it happen.

I don't really know what happened.

I only know that there was someone in the wood with me. I could feel him. It was a presence, but not the presence from the church. It was smaller, darker, more earthy. A man, I felt, some kind of man. Someone very old. He was behind me, I could feel it, but when I turned he was still behind me. I saw nothing at all, but I felt him, all the way through the wood, all the way through until I reached the stile at the other end, as if I had summoned him. As if the words had summoned him to me.

I am old enough now that I do not expect to understand much that happens in this world. But I still walked as fast as I could until I reached the path along the edge of the sands.

In church, sometimes, I see Anya, sitting quietly in the corner. Her swan neck is bowed in prayer, the white light is on her white hair. She is still, as she always will be now, until we meet again, if we do, if anybody does. I watch her. I want her to turn and give me that look. I want her to smile at me one last time. She never turns. But it is fine. Love is a practice, and so is grief. God wastes nothing.

My heart is smitten down and withers like grass, so that I forget to eat my bread.

But what do I sense in the wood? Because it was not only that time I felt it. That was six weeks ago, that first experience. Since then I have experienced this presence four times, and each time it is closer to me, it seems. It is something very old. It is something very old and uncaring. It wants something from me, but it does not care for me. Each time it is closer to me. Each time I walk faster and faster towards the sands.

It would be possible to believe I simply was an old man remembering his childhood fear of bramble thickets and dark paths. But it is not only the wood.

Four times I have felt that presence. And each time, later, I have seen the Angel.

I should perhaps be more precise. Really, I have not seen anything. Not clearly, not with my eyes. If I were to try and show anyone else, I doubt they would see what I see. I think they would see an old man who should wash his clothes more often, who usually has no milk in the house, who sometimes forgets to pay his electric bill. They would see an old man who should be in sheltered accommodation, for his own good. These would be the same people who drive their silver cars up on to the pavement and lock their doors against the moon. These would be the same people who can sit through a church service and feel nothing at all.

After church, I walk home. I have never driven. There is no need. Around here there are footpaths everywhere. Through the woods, over the commons, across the sands. The paths across the sands are hazardous. There are bones under there from each century there have been humans here. I never walk across the Bay, but I do not need to. From the churches I visit to my small terrace, the distance is barely more than two or three miles. I try to avoid the roads. The roads are so busy now.

I try to avoid home also, if I can. I can make tea, I can cook white fish and warm beans. I can sleep, and wake. I can even make the bed, if I want to, though I rarely do now. Anya used to care how things looked, and so I would care too. Without her, there is nobody to care, and nobody to look. Sometimes I will try to clean, but I don't usually get as far as I had planned to. I don't care if there is dust in the corners, or spiders on the ceiling. The smell doesn't bother me. It is not my business. A house is not a home without a woman in it, and I do not like tea without milk.

I go out a lot. I stay out. After the church, sometimes a pub for lunch. Sometimes I will sit on the promenade at Grange and watch the sky. I will watch the ducks around the lake, and the children feeding them. I like to sit by the old lido and remember it before it was ruins. We used to swim there, a lifetime ago. It was so cold you would feel alive afterwards for days.

Mostly, I like to walk. Walking is what we do in this land when we want to think, when we want to move beyond ourselves. Walking is our form of worship in this island, it is our practice, whether we know it or not. There is no reason to head anywhere. Walk empty, and something will find you. Our roads here were made by walking, not driving. This is a land of drove roads and pilgrim routes. We once were walkers, and will be again.

I came out of the wood, that first time, and down to the shores of the Bay. The mist was on the waters, hanging above them, moved by them, a weft of white air on the loom of the sea.

Then I heard the siren.

From the pier and the roadways the sound rang out: the bore was coming. I love to stand on the shores of the Bay and watch the bore approach. The silver line of water comes in steadily from the open sea, from beyond the windfarms and the forts, and it seems so slow but no-one could outrun it. It comes at you, suddenly faster now, and then it is foaming against the pier struts and the railway embankments and the stone walls under the quayside shops. There is nothing else like it. It is water moving as water should, as only water can.

In his hand are all the corners of the earth.

The bore did not look like that this time, because of the mist. I couldn't see the line of water. Instead, I heard it; I heard its surging breath below the siren, heard it move down towards where I stood. But all I could see was the mist, gently dancing over the rushing waters. The mist, grey-yellow now, the colour of the sand beneath it.

And then, in the mist, something else.

It was nothing, in a way; someone else might have seen it and moved on. As the mist moved with the bore, it brought with it, it created and fanned, what seemed to be a shape at its heart. It was like a clot of mist, as if the moist air were coagulating into a form. This clot of cloud at the heart of the cloud, far out in the Bay, dancing on the bore, it was yellow, gold, it emerged as something almost solid, then melted away again and then reformed. In the wood, I could feel a presence but I never saw it. Out in the Bay, in the mist that day, I could see a presence but I could not explain it, or define it. It was delicate, as if it could be blown away by a gust of wind or a sceptical word. But it was there. Some gold-yellow thing of clotted mist and sand and wind, writhing, dancing across the waters toward me like a pagan goddess with spears, swords, axes in her hands.

I am old enough now that I do not expect to understand much that happens in this world.

I have watched, and am even as it were a sparrow, that sitteth alone upon the house-top.

Four times now I have felt the presence in the wood. Four times now, later, far out on the sands, I have seen the Angel. Each time I have seen them, they have been closer to me. Each time, I have felt their presence more intensely.

The last time was this morning.

At the service this morning I did not feel like applauding. I don't know why. I feel that I wasn't paying attention. It wasn't the vicar's fault. I thought of Anya, as I always do in the pews where we once sat together; but I thought too of the figure in the woods and of the Angel and of what seemed to be coming toward me. There was nothing I could have pointed anyone towards. Through all of it, I have felt strangely calm. Somehow, it is not unusual. When you go out walking, things will come to meet you. It is not your work to explain them.

Ten minutes ago I walked out of the woods. This time, this last time, I almost felt like I saw something as I turned, hurrying. Some flash of light, some shape. Not quite a man. Taller. Older. Standing still, upright. Standing still, but hunting. From the corner of my eyes I saw his form. It was the old form, the old shape.

Now I am standing on the sands, waiting for the siren. It is late November. The trees are black and stark now, the sky crystal blue, and the mist is upon the face of the waters. I am waiting for the siren. The bore is due.

Anya and I would come here sometimes and watch the bore together. I would put my arm around her those last years, when she was so thin, and I would say, *I have you. I am here.* And she would say, *I know.*

We made a life, she said to me, once. *We made a life, and I am proud of it. I am proud of you.* When she smiled, I think, it would bruise me somewhere, and the bruise would take weeks to heal and I would not want it to.

I am not the only one on the beach this morning. The sands around the Bay are never crowded, but they are rarely empty. A few hundred yards to my right, down towards Grange, a woman is running her dog, throwing something for him to plunge in to the waters and retrieve. She is always here, with her black dog, lunging into the salt. To my left, over towards the great Kent estuary, a family is wandering the tideline. A man, a woman, two small children. These people will be here forever.

Behind me, the trees. Far beyond, the fells, snow-capped. When I was a boy, they looked the same. The people change, the mountains do not.

Beneath my feet, the sand is rumpled and raked in circling patterns like an Ouroboros, like the eye of God, like Patrick's exile of the snakes. My shoes are scuffed. Now that I look, I see that the laces are untied.

I am become like a pelican in the wilderness, and like an owl that is in the desert.

The siren begins. I look up.

The bore takes perhaps five minutes to reach this point once the sound begins. As before, I cannot see the line of water because of the yellow grey mist, now beginning to snake and curl and clot as the water rushes below it towards the place where sand meets soil. I watch. I stand rooted and I watch and keep watching and I hear. I begin to hear the water as the line of it rolls towards me. I smell the salt.

I step forward into the curling mist. I begin to walk out across the sands, across the shifting brown and silver sands, through the clots of cloud and out toward the sea.

And there she is. Out there, far out, I see her begin to coalesce above the water. In the arms and fingers of cloud, in the smoke-like curling of this blanket of sea fog, as the bore heads towards me, as the sound gets louder, stronger, I see her, my Angel. And she sees me. Her shape is clearer now, though it has no boundaries, it never settles, she is flow not object, process not event. Whatever she is, she is not human. The dog walker makes no noise to my right, the family to my left say nothing. She has only come for me.

I continue walking out across the sands, through the mist, towards the bore. Now she has turned and she moves towards me. The Angel approaches, she covers miles and years in seconds and the sound of the water now is everything. The bore must be near. I cannot see in this cloud. I feel the sands below me shift. And here she is now, this movement, this creature of cloud and form, here she is before me.

I turn and look back towards the shore. The cloud parts and I see him standing at the edge of the wood.

I turn back to her, in the cloud, in the water. Now I will be eaten. The sound of the water is more than a sound now, it is the place, it is the second of time it exists in. It is roaring around me. I am shaken. I cannot see my feet.

I will be eaten, now.

For my days are consumed away like smoke, and my bones are burnt up as it were a fire-brand.

But I am not eaten. I cannot paint a picture for you. I cannot tell you what it is or what it looks like. Only that it seems she holds out her hand, and that I know her and always have. She seems to hold out her hand and move towards and beyond and through me, and between the wood and waters, then, something happens that is so small, so untouchable, that it becomes everything.

Sand, water, cloud, light.

I have long given up pretending to understand anything. It is alright. She is here, and it is alright. Nobody else sees. We are alone, and she has come for me and nothing is what I thought it was.

And then I am standing on the sand, alone, and the water is gone and my shoes and trousers are soaked and the day is still as beauty.

They shall perish, but thou shalt endure.

And I must go home.

The Husband and the Wife Go to the Seaside

By Melissa Wan

T he husband and the wife arrived at their cottage on the coast. Both were ready for a change and told themselves this time away was the beginning. The night was moonless. Pulling up to the gate they saw that their cottage – mid-terraced in a row of holiday homes – was the only one with its lights still on, shining into the dark. The wife said it looked exactly like the pictures. When the husband stepped out of the car to unlock the gate, she smiled at him as he turned back, before realising he wouldn't see her in the glare of headlights.

Approaching a house with all the lights on made the wife feel like an intruder, but the husband turned the key and edged her in with his hand on the small of her back. Everything awaiting them seemed exactly as they had expected.

"Nice of them to leave the heating on," said the husband, peering into the dining room. The wife walked upstairs, half expecting to come upon another couple in their bed. Instead the towels and blankets were neatly folded, not a crease in sight. Downstairs, the husband had left a trail into the sitting room, his brogues kicked off and suitcases abandoned in the hallway. He was flopped into an armchair – the best one, she noticed – and tapping into his phone.

"After this we're turning them off," he said, "and I'll find a place to hide them."

"Do we have to?" said the wife. "What if I need to get in touch with you?"

The husband looked up from his phone with raised eyebrows. "You said we needed some time away, so that's what we're doing. It's two weeks."

The wife nodded and turned into the kitchen. She found a gift basket from the owner on the counter, with a handwritten card reading *Welcome to Arnside.*

"We can always eat these," she held up a tin of spaghetti hoops.

"What a bizarre thing to leave," said the husband.

"They're nostalgic," she said. "We used to have the alphabet ones. I'd eat them from my bowl which had the alphabet around the side."

The husband stood beside her and she told him he could heat them up.

"No thank you," the husband took out a packet of shortbread and sat down at the dining table. "We never ate anything tinned."

The wife put the tin back into the basket and sat across the table from the husband. She kept mistaking the tap of a twig on their kitchen window for a knock at the door, and every time she would snap up her head. She could hear the husband chew above the thin vibration of the fridge.

"It's so quiet here," she said.

"That," said the husband, "is the sound of having left it all behind."

The wife turned on the television, glad for the false laughter of a studio audience. She asked if they could go to the fish and chip shop tomorrow, and the husband said she could do what she wanted.

"It's what I've been dreaming about," said the wife. "The drip of all that chip fat."

The husband unfolded his paper and raised it to hide his face. On the cover, the wife read the headline: *Body Found in River Bela*. The photograph beneath was of the river – static in black-and-white – and didn't show the body. She remembered they'd crossed it on their drive through Milnthorpe and stopped to walk over the footbridge. Her eyes widened at the thought of a corpse drifting cold and stiff below their feet.

"What's that noise?" she asked, looking up at the window.

"What noise, darling?"

"The house... it's breathing."

The husband told her not to let her imagination run away with her. Turning up the volume, she stared blankly at the screen as the husband turned the page.

When the wife got into bed, she left her light on for longer than usual. Her eyes would lose their place in her book, find it again and read the same sentence over. She wore her new satin nightclothes spotted with pink roses and slipped herself beneath the quilt. When the husband came in wearing his flannels, he kissed her on the head, switched off his light and turned away onto his side.

"It was times like these," the wife read, "when I thought my father, who hated guns and had never been to any wars, was the bravest man who ever lived." She turned to look at the back of the husband's head. She could detect where his hair was beginning to thin. She closed her paperback, sipped at her water and turned off her reading lamp.

"Goodnight," she said.

The husband made a noise with his throat.

"It'll be nice to be here, won't it? To refresh."

The wife adjusted her pyjamas until an audible sigh came from the husband's side and she was still. There was a skylight in the ceiling through which, on her back, she watched the drift of cloud.

In the morning the husband and the wife were woken by the sound of drills. A team of builders were busy on the scaffolding around the front of the house next door.

The husband retrieved his phone to email the cottage owner, who wrote back to tell them it had been on the website. Indeed, he found the small print, illegible until he magnified the page: "From the mid August until January there will be building work next door. Some noise and disruption may be experienced."

"You mean it's going to be this loud the whole time?" asked the wife.

The husband said they would be out most days anyway, and told her not to look when he put the phone away.

The house looked tired in daylight, its walls and surfaces more grey than white. On the website, the sitting room was described as historic, but the bookcase was stuffed with second-hand romance novels and the wife knew the throws were bought in Ikea.

"It could do with a lick of paint," she said, to which the husband replied that this was what they called 'shabby chic'.

The wife boiled the kettle and took her cup of tea upstairs. She sat by the window, looking down onto the street beyond their front garden. Since the husband had claimed the armchair, the wife contented herself either with the sofa in the sitting room, or this chair with the view. From here she could see the labourers moving back and forth. When the bronzed arms of a worker caught her eye, her cup stopped before her lips. His muscles shifted as he hoisted a plank onto his shoulder, and he walked with extraordinary confidence for somebody so high up. When he shifted the board from his shoulder, she glimpsed the dark growth of hair beneath his arms.

After breakfast, through which the drills whined and the wife overcooked the eggs, she left the house arm in arm with the husband. The promenade was a few hundred metres away, a mixture of express supermarkets, small-town cafes and upscale boutiques. To walk from the pub on one end to the chip shop on the other took about five minutes.

This morning a layer of cloud turned the sky white and they passed groups of elderly ramblers in fleeces and walking boots.

The husband greeted people as though he knew them, shaking their hands because it was a small town, and as he said, things are done differently in small towns. The wife smiled but kept her eyes squinted on the mudflats, knees knocking as gusts of wind blew up her skirt. Luckily she'd packed a jumper but eventually she had to ask if she could buy a pair of trousers from the shop.

"I did tell you," said the husband, handing her their credit card.

The husband waited in the pub, sitting down with a pint as the wife closed the changing room door. It was a shop for ramblers and the wife looked so ridiculous in the waterproof pants and sandals that she reluctantly bought a pair of their cheapest walking boots and asked to wear both immediately.

Handwritten labels told her the fleeces were made from a flock of rare Woodland sheep, farmed only a few metres away. There was a tin of Werther's Originals on the counter and the wife thought for an instant it was all staged, as though if she opened a wrapper she would find a piece of folded card inside.

"You know there are rambling groups here," said the shopkeeper. "And Cedric does cross-bay walks. They're very popular."

The wife took her receipt, saying she wasn't a big walker.

Arriving at the pub – hoping to have lessened the effect of the mismatch by taking down her hair – she found the husband talking to a crowd of older women at a table outside. Their faces were browned with sun, hair silvered with streaks of black, and their trekking poles were stacked against the wall beside them. Amid this crowd, the wife thought the husband looked distinguished. She had the notion of him as a stage actor well known for performing Shakespeare. His jeans and jacket of cornflower blue were the precise balance of casual and chic; his hair peppered just enough to make the wife in her present state feel humiliated.

She went inside to order half a pint – hoping the women might leave – but when she came out, they had surrounded the husband and all were laughing together. The wife approached the group from the side and handed him their card, excusing her appearance by gesturing to her trousers and explaining you couldn't buy anything normal in there. The ramblers cackled and stuck their legs into the air, telling her she was one of them now.

"You'll have to come on our next walk," said one.

"We have a pole you can borrow," said another.

"I have a spare coat that should fit."

"Oh no," blushed the wife, looking at her husband, "This was just for the cold."

The ramblers shook their heads, the dark sunglasses on their headbands like so many rows of additional eyes.

"She says that now," said one.

"Just wait 'til you've been in them pants a few days," said another.

"You won't be able to get her out of them!"

They all screamed with laughter. The husband told the wife that one of the women had a partner who'd also gone to Cambridge.

"They were different years of course," said the woman, "But I'm sure they'll have lots to gossip about."

"Isn't that a coincidence?" said the wife. "If I met anyone from my old poly we wouldn't have anything to say."

The women chuckled and the husband said his wife had a wicked sense of humour, at which she smiled and supped her porter.

"How did the two of you meet?" asked one.

"We both teach at the same school," said the husband.

The wife said, "He's history and I'm English."

"Luckily we're all English here," she replied.

"Although we are getting a lot of Poles," whispered another.

"And not the right kind!" They lifted their sticks and roared.

They began to talk about property, how dead the market was, and conversation turned to their partners. They said their

44

other halves went fishing whilst they walked and enjoyed their freedom. In the evenings the two groups came together to watch the sunset.

"Turner said Margate had the best skies in Europe, but he'd probably never been to Arnside."

"Archie has the perfect viewing spot. Always comes with Prosecco."

"He'd be happy to pull out extra chairs."

The wife said they needed to catch the next episode of a show she was addicted to, and the women told them it would have to be next time. Luckily a siren sounded and the group was up, downing their pints and saying they were going to catch the bore.

"You'll want to meet Archie," said one to the husband.

"He'll take you canoeing," said another.

"We're surprised you haven't met him already," and they laughed for a final time.

When they left, the husband finished the wife's porter and said he was going to see the bore from the pier. The wife had no choice but to follow, the sound of the women's laughter still ringing in her ears.

"They seem to have their routine worked out," she said. "Too much activity for us though, don't you think?"

Although sunbathing in this weather was nonsensical, a young girl lay on the jetty in two pieces of red string, magazines heaped beneath her towel. Passers-by smiled when they looked at her, zipping up their parkas against the wind. The siren sounded again as she tucked in her breasts to flip onto her front. The wife began to comment, but the husband had walked on.

She came up by his side and asked him when the tide was coming in.

"That was it," said the husband.

The wife looked down at the water. It wasn't more than a couple of centimetres high and was the same dirty grey as the sky.

"Oh," she said.

"You know this is one of the only places it happens on the whole planet?"

By the time she turned around, the husband had walked on again. She saw him on the promenade, tufts of hair blowing in the breeze, his shoulders lifted in a shrug to the question they were both asking.

The wife quickly learned to occupy herself as she saw fit, and by the end of the first week, both of them were spending much of their time apart. The wife decided she didn't have to cook if she didn't want to, had eaten at the chip shop twice and tried hard to leave mess she could avoid clearing up. A sock in the kitchen, hardened crusts on her plate, a used toothpick on the doily. It wasn't long before the husband was out every day, fishing with the Archie mentioned at the pub. The husband brought bait in exchange for borrowing his equipment, and in the morning the wife chopped pieces of chicken into food bags, wincing at the raw flesh between her fingers. She kissed the husband goodbye and shut the door behind him.

There was a gift shop near one end of the promenade which sold artisanal ice cream. The wife began to frequent it every day and this was the furthest she would walk. Most mornings she darkened her lips, did her hair in a French twist, and looked only at the top half of her body in the mirror. As she walked she often drew the gazes of men. Today a crowd in shooting jackets tipped their hats as she passed, and the wife smiled before she sauntered on.

Passing the pier, she could never spot the husband. The anglers were all old and portly, flat caps pulled over their thinning hair. She continued to walk until the gift shop with its lurid blue paint, tacky postcards and baskets with multi-coloured hats out front. When she ordered her rum and raisin, the shop assistant asked if she was in Highbank. Initially the wife forgot this was indeed the name of their house, but when she remembered, she shook her head and said no, she was staying with relatives in Milnthorpe.

"I was sure it was you," said the woman, wetting her scoop and rolling a perfect globe. "Marda said she'd bumped into you and your husband last week at the Albion."

The wife smiled but stayed quiet. When the woman rolled another, she asked, "Doesn't your husband go fishing with Arch?"

At last the wife said that yes, he did.

"They'll have him in a canoe soon," said the woman, licking the end of her finger. "Archie has an adventurous nature." She smiled and pushed a plastic spoon into the ice cream. "You're not as talkative as your husband, are you?"

The wife thanked her and told her to keep the change.

"You want to be careful on that sand. It's not like normal beaches. Some people have sunk up to their waists."

The wife walked down the prom and stopped at a bench facing the sands. Sometimes big crowds crossed the flats, but today it was empty. She sat and licked her ice cream as the train rolled in across the viaduct. The promenade was quiet, and she suddenly became conscious of being a woman alone. The hairs on the back of her neck began to stand on end when a crowd of seagulls flocked down to the bench beside her and sent her to her feet in surprise. They struck at the scraps in a polystyrene box with their polished yellow beaks, and their shrieks followed her as she rushed away.

When the wife got home, the husband was in his armchair. He had fallen asleep with his phone on his knee, and when he stirred, she asked what he was doing. He sat up and, rubbing his eyes, said he only took it out to quickly use the map.

"Well then I'd like to use mine, quickly," she said.

He looked at the wife's trousers. "You've not been walking around in them all day?"

The wife ignored him and said she wanted to talk to somebody she knew. "And I want to meet Archie. I'm not sure why I haven't been introduced already, everyone else seems to think he's really something."

The husband sat up. "You'd honestly have nothing to talk about."

"Because I didn't go to Cambridge?"

"He's not Cambridge," the husband said, then mouthed "Oxford."

"God knows you lot think you're a breed apart," she said.

"If you want to know the truth, he did want us for dinner but I fibbed and told him you get migraines."

"You told him I get migraines?"

"It rolled off my tongue."

"Your tongue again," said the wife. "It's always going places you didn't intend it to."

The husband told the wife there was no need to be nasty. He walked into the kitchen and said she could do what she wanted, but that they were a bunch of bores when they got together.

"And how do you know that?"

"I can imagine."

"I suppose you go on imaginary fishing trips too?"

The husband poured himself a glass of wine and told her everybody knew you had to go to the river to catch the real fish. "And it's terribly boring when you play the suspicious wife."

"That's one way to shift the blame."

"Why does there always have to be someone to blame?"

"It's just it doesn't seem to matter what time we go to bed, or what I wear... none of this," she motioned at the room, "seems to make any difference. You always say it's because we're busy or because you're stressed – "

"Well it doesn't help does it?"

The husband walked up the stairs and left the wife to listen to the clock, ticking in time with the thump of her heart.

The following day the wife was up and out as soon as the sun had risen. The night had been restless and full of dreams in which she'd driven home early, letting the husband take the train. In the morning she tried to find the key to the cupboard where her phone was locked. She gave up when she realised she didn't have a clue as to where the husband might hide it.

One of the cafes on the prom was open and the wife sat there for much of the morning, drinking a cup of tea that was refilled before she bought another, the paperback untouched in her lap. People came in and out, dotting the tables around her. A couple arrived and sat by the window, on the same side as each other. The wife watched them share a black forest gateau. The boy refilled the girl's teacup whenever it was empty and let her have the cherry. The wife wanted a drink. Young couples in love, she thought as she paid the bill, have no regard for the rest of us.

The wife spent the rest of the afternoon moving between one pub and the other. Once or twice the crowds inside recognised her and said hello, but she feigned deafness as best she could and they soon left her alone. She buried her face between the pages of her book, never reading a word. As the afternoon drew on, she lifted her eyes to watch the ramblers as they returned from their walks, skin ruddy with cold, mouths lifted at the corners. Why is nobody here unhappy? she thought, and ordered another beer.

These were wonderfully cloudy, golden beers and she soon lost count of what number she was on. The wife always ordered porter around the husband as, for an unknown reason, it was the only beer he approved of her drinking. At first she'd tried to work out if he was joking – and she suspected he was – but in the end it felt easier to grow to like it than mention it again.

"Everything okay for you?" The waiter came out of nowhere. The wife looked up through hazy eyes and said yes thank you everything was just fine. The potted shrimp smelled delightful but no, she'd just finish her beer.

"You want to set off home." He took her empty glass. "Got a feeling the weather's going to turn. One minute it's clear, and then..."

When the wife stood and drained her bitter, she felt glad for her thick boots. By the time she got home, the workmen were packing up, shutting the doors to their vans. The lad who'd had his shirt off stood by the road, smoking. He was young enough to remind the wife of some of the older boys she taught.

"Couldn't spare one, could you?" She stopped as she walked past, feeling bolder for the alcohol in her bloodstream.

He fished into the pocket of his tracksuit bottoms and pulled out his packet, flicking open the top. She took one and asked for a light. He had on his poker face, keeping his mouth shut to feign indifference around the men, who had all fallen still. The wife took a drag, feeling warmth as she inhaled. Breathing out, she looked at him. She couldn't say if he was good looking, he was just young.

"It's going to rain," she said. "Don't want to get wet."

She walked away, conversations starting up again as she opened her gate. She bent to untie the laces of her boots on the doorstop, cigarette in mouth, and didn't look back when they drove by.

The wife knew the house was empty before she put her key in the lock. She supposed an evening alone would be welcome. Kicking off her walking boots, she walked through the house and turned on all the lights. In the sitting room she stood and looked at the husband's armchair: pristine white, unruffled. The wife lowered herself into it and put her feet on the table, smoking until she got to the stub. She'd missed that wave of calm, being able to watch the smoke drift and curl in the air. She turned on the television to murmur in the background and decided to eat the tin of spaghetti hoops.

As she was alone, she slurped and tried to make a noise when she burped, letting the thick arms of the chair hug her into a stupor.

Before she fell asleep – with the heat and beer, stomach full – she watched through narrowed eyes something on the television about single mothers. The screen showed a woman with smudged mascara, crying into her tissue. Afterwards, the wife wouldn't remember whether or not she had dreamt this.

When the wife woke, it was dark and raining. Something loose rattled on the roof. There was a chill in the air and the rain had left dirty streaks on the windows. The tide was in, glossy black with gulls hovering low over its surface.

She called out for the husband but no reply. The clock read quarter to midnight. She looked at the grandfather clock in the hallway to make sure it was right. The wife couldn't help thinking of the headline on his paper the day of their arrival. She imagined him washed away in a river flood, being sucked into the sand and buried alive. The wife believed in premonitions. She forever told of how out of sorts she felt the day before Princess Diana's death, of how she had found hints everywhere: a burned-out car on the motorway, her niece's plastic crown snapped in two. *It's like something was telling me*, she told her sister. *I could feel it.* She'd had the same intuition of fear when they first approached the village, its streetlights blinking from afar, the only sound the low murmur of their car.

She walked into the kitchen to pick up the paper by the bin, but there was no longer any headline about a body in the river. The picture was of a woman crying, inky lashes running into the white of a tissue. The picture felt familiar, but the wife was sure she hadn't seen it on the front page. She checked the date, and it was the same Westmorland Gazette of the day they'd arrived. Flicking through, she found no reference to the death she was certain she'd read about.

"Where is he?" she breathed. The thunder answered in a long, ominous roll, sending the wife rushing up the stairs.

"Please, please," she said. Accidents happened, she knew, the line between life and death thin as a hairline crack. All it took was a step in the wrong direction.

The air in the bedroom was chill and she noticed the draught was coming from the open window. She pulled it shut, rain hammering on the skylight like hail. She was glad she'd turned on all the lights and noticed, for the first time, a framed photograph of a river by the bed. As she leant in closer, she knew the name she'd find before she read it. Typed in silver, glinting as she approached, it read 'the River Bela'.

A gurgling erupted from the bathroom. The wife walked into the corridor with her eyes wide, and put her hand on the door. When she pushed it open, the toilet was belching, throwing up sludge from below the surface. She slammed the door shut behind her and despite herself, rushed into the bedroom and pulled the husband's jumpers from his suitcase. Clutching the sleeve of one, she fell to the floor and closed her eyes. A flash of lighting illuminated the bedroom and she pulled the wool over her head.

Her thoughts shifted between possibilities. For a moment, she wondered if the husband wasn't playing a joke. He could be somewhere in the house, maybe even with Archie. Perhaps they came back when she was asleep and, knowing her fears, had cracked open the window and conspired to have a laugh at her expense. She wouldn't have put it past him. She tried to convince herself the husband had stayed with Archie and those laughing crones. Perhaps he'd found something there he liked. She wouldn't have put that past him either.

Eventually the rain quietened, and all other noise stopped. The wife was stiff when she stood and walked to the bathroom. The toilet was silent now but it looked like someone had hurled mud into the bowl, and much of the floor was wet. The wife excavated the cabinet for her husband's sleeping pills and swallowed two to send her out cold for the rest of the night. To stop me worrying, she thought, though she knew you didn't need to worry after the fact.

The wife crawled fully dressed between the covers and swaddled her head in the duvet.

The next day, the sky had cleared and the wife was relieved to hear the workmen. She called out, knowing already the husband wasn't home. His jumper was limp on the floor and she felt momentarily embarrassed by last night's conduct.

She walked down the stairs and peered out of the front window. The potted plants were green and swollen with rain. The lad from yesterday was smoking by her gate, and he looked over when she opened the door. The wife gestured at him to come through. He threw his cigarette to the floor, hitched up his jogging bottoms and opened the latch. She told him there was a problem with their bathroom and the toilet had kept her up with its noise.

"You couldn't have a look, could you?" She watched his eyes move over her face, to her lips and back when she spoke. "Quickly," she said, letting him in and closing the door. She told him it was upstairs and watched him climb the stairs, never looking back to see if she was following. He rattled around, flushing the toilet a few times before shouting down it was the storm which had blocked it. He spoke with an accent, as the wife had expected. She looked at her reflection in the hallway mirror, at her knotted hair and crumpled clothes, and told herself she was something fuckable. There was a long pause in which she waited with her ears pricked up. She realised she could hear him taking a piss. The sound travelled down the stairs, full of intent, more direct than that of the husband.

When the wife appeared in the doorway, he turned to look at her. He shook it out and put it back into his trousers.

"You're alone?"

She nodded as he walked up to her, the smell of sweat.

"I've seen your man. He likes to wear tight jackets."

She told him the husband was no longer here.

"Where is he?"

The wife looked at his arms, all bone and muscle, lined with fine veins.

"I'm a widow," she said, running her fingers along the tiles as though trying to feel the effect of that word through the stone. "You know I played with Polish boys when I was a girl. For a while I pretended I was one."

He told her she couldn't be from Poland.

"They don't know that," she said. "It's harder for them to recognise your class if you pretend you're foreign."

He turned away from her and stuck his hands under the tap, splashing water onto his face and running his fingers through his hair. The wife didn't move until he looked at her in the mirror and said, "So you're a widow. What do you want me to do about it?"

The husband came home that afternoon. As though the wife had known, she'd sprayed the hallway and bedroom with air freshener. She was curled into his armchair and didn't hear the door when he came in.

The wife thought he looked exactly as he had before he died.

"What are you doing in my chair?" he said.

"I was waiting for you."

"You've got other chairs to do that in."

The wife stood. She noticed a smear of mascara on one of the cushions and turned it around.

The husband walked up the stairs and the wife prepared lunch. She wondered what he might say about the state of the bedroom; the sheets tangled and his clothes on the floor. She knew he wouldn't say anything.

The wife hardboiled two eggs and crushed them into glops of mayonnaise. She used the stale bread she'd bought yesterday, or was it the day before? She sliced the sandwiches in half and slid them into food bags, then sat by the window to wait. Although she couldn't see them from down here, she could hear the workmen; an occasional call, a tool being dropped.

The wife and the husband walked along the promenade until they reached the pier. The husband ignored everyone who greeted them and the wife answered with a meek hello. They took the steps hewn into the side of the pier down to the sand. The tide was out and the wife perched on a large boulder beside the walkway while the husband continued to stand. He didn't touch his food, and after a bite the wife realised she didn't want hers either.

"Where did you fish yesterday?" she asked.

"The river," he said. "We went canoeing."

The wife had known that. On the River Bela. She watched the husband walk lightly across the wet sand, his footprints fading as he moved.

"Did you catch anything?" she said, and the husband shook his head.

"Probably just a cold."

He smiled and the wife's face crumpled. She remembered the girl in her bikini and thought about how she too had wanted a real beach. You could hardly call it one when you couldn't slide your toes between the grains, or make castles that washed away with the waves. The wife said she hated rambling, that she never wanted to come here in the first place, feeling she could say that now.

"Everything here is grey," she said. "And this place was supposed to make us better."

"You don't think we're better?" asked the husband.

The wife stood and grasped a pebble between her fingers, mottled and brown. When she threw, the stone missed the husband and landed behind him in an ungraceful plunk. Every time, the pebbles fell in wet thuds a few feet behind him.

She turned away to look into the white of the sky and the point at which it met the bay. There was a thin, horizontal line between one world and the other.

"What now?" the wife breathed.

She felt a pebble sail past her ear. It skimmed the surface of a channel in the sand, touching the water four, five, six times before it disappeared. She stopped still as another danced across the shallow. They seemed to skip on forever.

When she turned to look at the husband, he had his eyes fixed on the line of the horizon, squinting at the light. There was a look on his face she had never seen before. The wife watched the elegant flick of his wrist and the stones as they flew through the air.

The pebbles, each time, became weightless.

A Kinder Light

By Bethan Ellis

Her name was Mrs Richardson, or at least that was the name she used around the time I came to know her, in the autumn just before she died. She had a room in one of those low Victorian terraces in the West End, the long undifferentiated streets that slope down gently from the seafront, and whose ageing owners offer bed and breakfast not from any natural gift for hospitality, but from a deeper understanding of the subtle grades of need, the spark of mutual knowledge that no longer clothes itself in kindness. We're all poor sinners here, the dusty vacancy signs say, and hold their tongue where other, better streets might state no DSS, no benefits. The owners cash the cheques and mash the tea and ask no questions, and a fry-up carries you a long way through the day.

I knew these former boarding-houses in the streets below the Bay, because I lived in one for several months, on a very temporary basis. I had found work with one of those small charities that flourishes like mushrooms then just as quickly disappears with a sharp frost, a change of government. My situation had become untenable and I had needed very much to leave; I reasoned that a seaside town where I knew not a single soul would suit me fine.

I had not been wrong. Nobody asked after my welfare or my secrets; the closest that I ever came to being questioned was one morning after coffee when one of the old ladies, I knew her afterwards as Nora, and quite kind, leaned in to me as we were washing up and asked in a sharp voice,

"Not married, then?"

The wine glass I was wiping underwater shattered and the suds inside the plastic bowl bloomed red; when I lifted my hands empty from the water there was a cut along my thumb, quite deep. I looked at it and for a moment couldn't understand what had just happened. Nora was all fuss and kindness, and when I was patched up to her satisfaction, she sat down with me and squeezed my hand.

"Don't you mind," she murmured. "Don't you mind."

Afterwards, when my two years on the Bay had come to seem a distillation of those hard, conflicted months before, and not the clean start that I imagined at the time, I wondered at the congregation's lack of curiosity. It is only now that I have settled for an ordinary compromise in another seaside town with its own slow tides of refugees and tourists that I have a sense of what it is to watch these people come and go, and wonder which, if any of them, might be worthy of your patience or your time.

And then I think of Mrs Richardson.

I joined the church below the Bay one morning quite by accident. It was a bright, blue day in August, the sky arched high over the seafront where I often walked and watched the water dance on mornings when I couldn't sleep. Too early for the smattering of day-trippers, and the streets were all still empty, or I thought they were until I saw a tidy band of women in their seventies, macs buttoned up, hair washed and set, moving down Regent Street with a steady purpose quite at odds with the warm day. I followed them, half lonely, half in love with the idea of myself as an astute observer, until they came to the side entrance of St Martin's, and one of them produced a key and they went in. I heard them lock the door again behind them, and I realised it was Sunday, and they must be in to make the teas before the service, or whatever it was old women did in musty-smelling rooms behind a church. I had passed it almost every day, a great low barn built for more prosperous or perhaps more certain times, squatting on a corner of the terraced streets, its size completely out of kilter with the rooftops gathered at its knees. It diminished them, the way an oil tanker makes trinkets of the houses near the harbour, houses that hide entire lives within their walls.

I sat down on the kerb outside the church and watched the seagulls squabble over last night's chips. The paper clapped and rattled in the quiet, and the casual savagery with which the seagulls fought for their fair share was so absorbing that I didn't hear the footsteps of the priest as he walked up and saw them off and gathered up the wrappings, bundling them underneath his arm and never mind the grease. The gulls squawked fury from the chimneys opposite as he nodded his good morning, turned and disappeared inside the church, only to reappear some moments later hauling back the big oak doors, making them fast against the breath of wind with heavy iron hooks.

"You'd better come in soon," he said. "We're on at eight."

I bent down and scratched my ankle, hid my face and didn't answer. My jeans were tight from all the home-cooked breakfasts, all the cheap meat and greasy eggs I couldn't bring myself to leave because I didn't want to seem ungrateful. I had not yet found somewhere to live.

"Well," he said, "you're welcome anyhow."

When I looked up, he was gone.

I sat another moment in the sun. The light, if I was honest, was what kept me there. The way it washed along the narrow streets on mornings just like this one, gently glancing through the tired windows, saved me from jumping on the next train back. There was a softness to its touch. A kinder light. I closed my eyes, rested my face into its warmth. Then the seagulls overhead were drowned out by a peal of bells, and in the sudden dazzle as I let the sun back in I stood up and somehow found myself outside the open doors, then walking through into the cooler darkness.

The air inside was thick with lavender and incense, and the sweet milk-chocolate smell of cloth and paper that had been shut in drawers and cupboards slightly damp. From a back room came the sound of coffee cups. I hesitated at the second set of doors, listening for a cue for me to enter. No sound came. I slipped into the nave and for a moment the great height of it surprised me, more space and air and daylight than the lazy sprawl of slate and glass suggested from outside. Where I expected heavy wooden pews there were rows instead of low, wide chairs, their seats and backs upholstered with red hessian, almost of all of them unfilled. Nobody turned round as I took my place towards the back, ready to escape; only the priest looked up from where he was busying himself with wine and silverware and nodded once. He was the same age as me, or younger, his eyes a touch too close together, giving his glance a dark intensity that perhaps he did not mean. I looked down, confused, and by the time I was prepared to brave his gaze again he had turned away, and was smoothing down the altar-cloth with practised hands.

The service, when it came, was amplified, and the speakers on the pillars gave his voice the quality of being overheard, the exact same weight and volume given to his every breath as to the liturgy. I found it difficult to concentrate on what he was doing at the front; the tinny whisper at my ear distracted me. Some of what he said I knew from school, from the service once or twice a year for which we formed two straggling reluctant lines and dawdled down the road towards the modern church, which didn't look like any of the pictures in our books and which, I now remembered, had also been St Martin's. There was a solemn colour to his voice that was different from the vague anxious encouragement I remembered from those services at school. He looked across the heads of his small congregation: the scattering of old women, the nervous-looking man in his late twenties, me. His focus lay beyond us, and I realised his performance would have been the same had there been no one in the church. The incense smell grew stronger, and while I had made a passing imitation of the others, rising in my seat and sitting down and kneeling just in time, when they rose and made their way down to the front I could not follow. I had not been confirmed, although for a moment I wanted nothing more than to receive communion, to put down all my questions as I knelt before the priest and open my mouth and let him place the wafer on my tongue, wipe the cup and offer me his wine and absolution. The light streamed through from the high windows and made haloes of the widows' faded hair.

Then they were all back in their places, as though nothing out of the ordinary had occurred. There was a hasty blessing and everybody rose to leave, or at least to hurry off into the hidden warren of church rooms to start the urn. The priest was waiting at the door to say goodbye. He was a little shorter than me, and as he took my hand in his warm grasp he caught my forearm an instant, and said,

"We'll be seeing you again."

There was no question in his voice, it was a statement of fact, the same inflection that he might have used to tell me it was raining. Except the sky outside was pale with sunlight now and it was still not quite nine o'clock. The whole service had taken no more than forty minutes.

I caught the habit, though. I found myself on those same streets the following Sunday, learned in time the words of the responses, and while it took some months for me to feel his warm palm damp and heavy on my forehead as he blessed and later christened me, the certainty he gave me with 'again' remained, a fixed point round which those doubtful weeks could coalesce and lay down shape and form. In hindsight, any kindness might have served that purpose; an oyster doesn't care what quality of grit finds its way into its soft insides. It only feels the hurt and forms the pearl.

Still, that tender need is what I recognised in Mrs Richardson. I caught the moment's hesitation as she tried to rise in time, the shaky panic when she followed us down to the altar rail, the way the young priest held her in his eyes. I knew by then that we were Anglo-Cath, not Roman Catholic; that peculiarly English stubborn compromise between the outward rituals and the inner doubt. Perhaps it would have been better for both me and Mrs Richardson if we had found a different church.

I saw her first in the eight o'clock Mass. It was late October and although the sky was weakening into morning the streets still held an aftertaste of night. I had gone along to ten o'clock communion enough times to learn there was a wider congregation than we scattered few at eight, but my instinct was for the brief simplicity of the early service, the hurrying through the ordinary magic of the bread that holds the body, the wine that keeps within its sticky sweetness the dark and iron tang of blood. I borrowed the impatience of the old women at the altar rail ahead of me, for whom the sacrament was both a necessary obligation and the point, and for whom the fripperies of prayer and liturgy were a waste of their scant days. If I had grown up in a different kind of family, I might have had another way of doing church, but as it was I followed the old women blind.

It was a blowy morning, the wind off the Bay had taken a few slates with it, and there was rubbish clattering round in the small yard all through the service. I still sat at the back, I liked the distance from the altar, and when Mrs Richardson crept in beside me I made it clear that I was making room for her. She had been taken badly by the wind, it left her white and breathless, although I later realised she was always far too pale. We had the lights on in the nave it was so dark outside, and when she untied her patterned headscarf, smoothed and folded it, the strangest thing: she had a yellow ribbon in her hair. As she settled in her seat, she patted the bow back into place, with the soft unconscious gesture of a little girl. That first time the service held her in its rhythms with a rapt attention that I recognised and missed now I belonged. She had of course been confirmed as a child, so she was free from the beginning to approach the altar, kneel and take communion. When we went back along the aisle towards our seats, in the quiet moment when I waited for the air around me to resolve itself in holiness, I was distracted by the ribbon. It had slipped forwards, and the ends of it were dangling in her eyes. I had to stop myself from leaning over and correcting it. She didn't seem to notice.

Some weeks afterwards we spoke for the first time, although it happened not to be at church, but on the seafront, in one of those dilapidated shelters where the broken glass allows the wind to scour out the tang of urine. I had walked out on an argument at work, my boss suddenly taking up far too much space in that awkward run of rooms above the betting shop. We were nearing Christmas and the money, it was clear, was drying up, and used as we were to the boom years when regeneration was measured by its outcomes, not its costs, none of us had any sense of what to do. The tide was going out, and above us leaned one of those longed-for skies where sunlight edges through a bank of cloud, and pours thick shafts of light onto the sea, and the idea of some bright heaven hangs a little closer to the earth. Then the wind stepped round, the cloudscape changed and I turned back inland. That was when I caught sight of her, huddled in the corner of the shelter in her flimsy dark-red coat, looking very small and very old, and at first I saw her only as one of the old women, widowed by time as much as accident and illness, and then she raised her hand to pat her ribbon into place, and I knew her: Mrs Richardson.

For all I'd spent my adult life in charities, I still found it difficult to strike up conversation with anyone in need. I loitered awkwardly in front of her, and for a moment I was twelve again, hanging round outside the bus-shelter where the big girls smoked, waiting for them to ask me to sit down.

"Lovely down here, isn't it?" I said at last, and she said nothing. Her eyes flickered up to mine, and then slid away and down and rested on her hands. That darting movement, shy and evasive, was one I came to pity and to love. "I don't see you down here so much," I tried again.

She shook her head as though to clear away whatever had been fogging up her brain. I think it was the first time I heard her speak.

"She didn't come," she said. "I'll meet you, I'll be there, that's what she said. I remember the date quite clearly. I wrote it down. I waited. On a bench just up the road from the estate. It wasn't kind."

"Who?" I asked. "Who didn't come?"

At first she didn't answer, only fiddled with her handbag.

"My daughter."

So you see, it wasn't my fault, all that happened, all that followed in those winter months; there was nothing deliberate in my misunderstanding her abandonment. If I let myself be gathered in by what she told me, saw an empty seat, it was because I thought there was a love or at the very least a kindness I could offer in its place.

"I'm sorry," I said, and took her hand, those small soft fingers, warm the way a child's might be, despite the cold.

"Not your fault," she said at last. "You weren't to blame."

We sat there in the shelter looking out towards the sea, a scrawl of ink that traced the far horizon.

She said, "I know you, don't I. Your face, I know your face. I see you at that church."

I answered yes, and she went on, as though I hadn't spoken. "They're a funny lot. All think they're better than they ought to be. But you, you're different. Not from round here."

I said no, and sketched out for her the version of events that I could share. I didn't touch on the unhappiness, I didn't know her well enough for that.

"I don't know how long I'll stay," I said.

"None of us do," she said. And then she turned to me, and her eyes darted up to mine and then away again, and they were wet from all the wind, I thought. "They told me that I'm dying," she said, and shook her head again, folded her hands. "She won't come."

I don't know what unformed idea of rescue I bore with me as I walked her home. Mrs Richardson was light still on her feet, and vague about exactly what was wrong with her, only she stopped when we were halfway down her street and held her side and closed her eyes and moaned a little. She didn't ask me in – the whole time that I knew her, I was never in her rooms, just that once after she died – and I remember being worried that she might not make it up the stairs, but then she closed the guesthouse door and disappeared, and I went back to our small offices to make peace with my boss.

Between the services of Remembrance that next Sunday I caught Fr John and asked him what to do. I was still a little wary of him, disliking the intent with which he listened, finding myself floundering for words, a sort of airless drowning. Perhaps he made me feel I ought to tell the truth.

"What do you want to do?" he asked, the emphasis on 'want'.

I didn't know. "I don't like to see her, on her own like that. Her daughter."

"You think she needs to see her? A family reconciliation?"

"I don't know," I said again, because I wasn't sure. I didn't like the sharpness in his voice. He had the faintest Ulster accent, and it gave a bitter edge to what he said, a sarcasm that perhaps he did not mean.

"Have you asked her?"

I asked her later on that day, and Mrs Richardson offered me her small evasive smile and said she didn't think that it was even possible, not now.

The year declined, and so did Mrs Richardson. She seemed to keep more to herself, as though whatever grew inside her was consuming all of her attention, and there were Sundays when I thought I'd maybe dreamed our conversation by the sea. Around this time I saw her walking on the sands, and I called her name and waved and tried to catch her, but although I followed her for quite some way, hugging the curved line of the sea wall, she remained too far ahead to hear me. She looked back once, and then seemed to accelerate, a small dark figure hurrying along the Bay and out of sight. Distances can be deceptive.

We held a Christmas dinner at the church, a celebration, if you could call it that, which was meant to offer festive comfort to the volunteers as much as to the old and lonely. We scrubbed and peeled and cooked and cleared, and passed around the sherry in the church hall, and cheap vodka in the kitchen just beyond, poured freely into thick green mugs of orange juice. Even Fr John took some vodka neat, and made a face, and drank it down. I kept myself quite busy with the washing up, enjoying the steam from the hot water on the windows and the carols on the radio, and the gentle tipsy feeling at three in the afternoon that was how we celebrated Christmas Day at home. It didn't matter that I wasn't there; I had told them I was needed, I couldn't get away, and it was partly true; I'd made myself a need in Mrs Richardson. I peeled off my rubber gloves and ran my hands under the cold tap then went through to see how she was doing. The tinsel had come down around the doorway and I pressed it back into the Blu Tack, and the congregation also seemed in need of mending, cracker-hats lopsided or removed, the remnants of the pudding going cold. Some of them were talking over *Once in Royal*, but for the most part the old women sat in silence, no more in common than geography and time, and a weakness for a drop more cream. What would they have talked about, if anyone had asked? Most of them had grown up here, knew the seafront in its crowded heyday, the years when all the terraces were spruce and washed, the windows polished bright with newsprint. The summers when you couldn't get a room. One woman pushed her sprouts around the plate and wept.

Mrs Richardson sat a little distant from the others, and ate with careful movements, pausing between mouthfuls to lay down her knife and fork and gaze into the empty air in front of her. I sat down and asked if she was enjoying her meal.

"Oh yes," she said. "It makes a change from eating on my own."

I wondered where she'd had Christmas last year and she made a dismissive gesture with her hand.

"I called," she said at last. "She didn't come. I'd have been better leaving well alone."

As she complained she dipped her head and looked up through her lashes and at once she was a little girl, putting out her lip and close to tears. I apologised, unsure what I'd done wrong. Something glinted at her ears and throat, and as she turned her face away I saw them clearly: rubies, lovely if old-fashioned, a necklace and a pair of matching earrings. The stones were heavy and pulled down at the old piercings in her lobes, made them into little slits. She caught me looking, and it was as though she, not I, had seen a thing she coveted.

"Lovely, aren't they?" she said, tucking a strand of hair behind her ear. "They were my mother's." She could see that I was thinking of her daughter and she shook her head. "They're not for her. She doesn't deserve them. Not now." She pushed her plate away. "I'm done."

In the run of days before the office opened up again in early January, I saw a lot of Mrs Richardson. I called round to the bed and breakfast where she lived, waited on the step in the sharp wind and walked with her along the seafront. Once we made it far enough to get a cup of tea. She told me more about her diagnosis, how it had spread, that Fr John had made arrangements for her at the hospice. She clutched my sleeve; despite the careful softness of her hands, there was a strength to her small grip. I thought of talons.

"I can't bear the thought, him going through my things. The priest. When I go in to the hospice, when I'm gone, would you mind?" She let the half-phrased question trail unfinished in the air, leaving me flattered and important in its wake. I said yes;

we were standing in the bitter cold and it was getting dark. She reached up quite unexpectedly and kissed me on the lips, the way a child might, without guile. Her breath carried a thick unhealthy sweetness, and it was that more than her words that made it true for me that she was dying.

She passed in early April after two months in the hospice. We had said prayers, thought of her often, although I'm not sure any of us visited, excepting Fr John. She told him that she didn't want to see me, sent on through him the key to her small room, although he forgot to pass it on until she'd died. I don't know what consoling hope she took from him, whether it was enough for him to hold her hand. We prayed for the condition of her soul.

I went to clear her things one Saturday. The house was empty, and there was nobody to witness my last kindness. The room was as she had said it would be: tidy, bed stripped, blanket folded at the foot of the thin mattress. There was a hairbrush lying on a little cloth beside the sink, and a tiny cut-glass bowl quite full of ribbons. She had said to leave the clothes, that Mrs Smith would take them to the hospice shop, but that I should gather up the rest, check she'd left nothing personal or valuable behind. There was so little left to take. I'd emptied out a cardboard box at work, but there was not enough of anything to fill it: a leather jewellery case, her rubies tucked inside, a clumsy knitted dog with cross-stitched eyes, the pearl-backed brush bearing its few white hairs, and on the night-table beside a little travel clock there lay a copy of *A Child's Garden of Verses* inscribed *To Lesley, from her Mother*. I picked it up and tucked inside the book there was a letter that had been folded and unfolded until the paper softened to a moth-like frailty that felt like it might fall to dust and ashes in my hands. I sat down on the bed and opened it. The handwriting was tentative and difficult to read. It was an invitation, dated several years ago, for Mrs Richardson to go and meet her grandchildren. They talked about her, the girls, and they would love so much to meet her. *Mum,* the message said, *I know you'll find it difficult, as I will, but I was still so small when I last saw you. I'm not sure I have your face right in my mind, except there's something of you in my eldest girl, she favours you.*

I folded up the letter carefully and tucked it back inside the book. Outside the window I could hear the seagulls calling lonely through the air. I felt a little sick. I had put my trust in Mrs Richardson and she had lied, or at least let me believe what was not true. I sat on her stripped bed until the front door went downstairs, another tenant letting themselves in. I gathered up a few last things and left.

I didn't go to church again until the morning of the funeral. I couldn't face the congregation, and I didn't want to speak to Fr John. In the end I had no choice. I had gone into the vestry to put the box down somewhere safe before the service, and he was in there with the smell of shoes and dust and ancient sweat. He was in his cassock, and he was smaller without the surplice he had reached up to put on; it was strange to see his waist. I asked where I should leave her things.

"Wherever you like," he said, "I'll find them afterwards." He turned to look at me for the first time. "The daughter came to see me yesterday." He seemed nervous, and I wasn't sure quite why; I had seen him lead at least three funerals since I had joined the church.

He said again, "The daughter." It wasn't nerves, more of a quiet agitation, one I recognised, but not from him, as someone waiting for a fight they're not yet sure they want to have.

"She said, she told me, Mrs Richardson abandoned her. Can you believe it?"

He shook his head. At first I thought it was the sadness of it all, but I was wrong.

"To make up such a thing. The way she died."

I held the box a little tighter in my arms. He was so young.

"She spoke to you," he said, "our Mrs Richardson?"

69

The words caught in my throat. The dust fell in the vestry, turning gently in the light, and the letter kept its counsel in the box. I shook my head. I didn't want to tell him anything.

"Only that she didn't come."

He nodded, half-whistled out a breath, readied himself.

"We'll see whether she makes it here today."

He pulled on his robes and left me standing in the vestry. I had meant to leave the box there for the daughter to collect, but now I changed my mind. Mrs Richardson had said the earrings weren't for her, and now I took her at her word, slipped them out of the slim case, and into a deep pocket of my bag. The thick cloth hanging on their pegs soaked up the noise.

The daughter was in the back row of the church. She was dressed not in black – the congregation in their funeral best all noted as they filed down to their seats towards the front – but in a navy jacket that would once have been expensive. I had not expected her to be there on her own. I sat across the aisle where I could see her face in profile, and set the box down on the seat beside me. She sat quite still, looking up at our stained glass. Even when the day is overcast, the little fragments glow, and on so bright a day the sea-light makes them shine, the colours rich and strange. There was a fumbling behind us and the heavy doors were opened wide, and for those few minutes all the noises from the street accompanied the coffin, carried up the aisle by four men from the funeral home. Then they closed the doors and we resumed our silence

The size of coffins still surprises me, how little space they take up in a church, and Mrs Richardson's was no exception. No flowers, she had said, but still the congregation had a wreath made for the box, yellow chrysanthemums, it would seem unkind not to have anything, and besides the florists do us a good price. There was nothing from the family. The service was, at first, quite unremarkable. The gathering he took from Timothy, 'We brought nothing into the world, and we take nothing out,' and then we all sang *Love Divine* and asked repeatedly for mercy. I don't recall the readings, only Fr John waiting with his head bowed in the pulpit, folded hands, breath rattling the microphone.

The sermon started quietly enough. The doubled 'nothing' had unsettled me. I lost myself in looking at the windows high above the altar, the blood-red halo round Our Lady's careful hair and the lilies underneath the angel's feet, and so I sensed rather than heard the change in the priest's tone, the way you know the tide has turned more from a moment's hush than any pattern in the waves. The congregation waited in their seats. He spoke of how our church had welcomed Mrs Richardson, given her a home these last few months.

"She told me just how much your kindness meant."

He paused; the congregation preened and dared to glance around.

"She came to live among us on her own," he said, "a woman quite abandoned by her family."

They held their breath.

The daughter sat quite still, her chin a little raised. She was paler even than her mother, the same light and sliding eyes now looking to the door, now turning back, determined to endure. He never let his gaze drift from her face. His version of her flickered in the air.

"I was with her at the end," he said, a different colour in his voice, a note of sorrow in amongst the righteous anger.

The daughter flinched.

"She told me just how much she missed her daughter, how she never gave up hoping that she'd come. All those last days she waited and she prayed, and I believe it brought a certain kind of comfort. I hope," he faltered here, his voice clotted and thick, "I hope that none of you may die alone."

He cleared his throat and stepped down from the altar. I couldn't look round at the daughter.

"Let us pray."

His voice dropped back into the familiar confiding murmur of his prayers. We listened and we echoed without thinking, *hear our prayer*. All around I felt the lively malice of the congregation, united by the venom of his sermon, for all that they had never suffered Mrs Richardson as one of them. They sat a little straighter in their seats.

She walked behind the coffin on her own. The organ maundered softly on, and I picked up the box and cradled its small weight against my hip. She was standing on the steps outside the door, looking a little dazed in the bright sunlight, as though she had been hit, and the blow was only now starting to register. The congregation flowed out through the doors and parted round her, turned and formed their little knots of gossip, electric with the words the priest had used. There was some delay before the crematorium, and the funeral cars stood idle in the street outside, the slick black paintwork giving back the sky. I walked over, introduced myself, said that I was sorry for her loss, I had been friendly with her mother – I hesitated to claim her for a friend – and that she'd asked me to gather up some personal effects and pass them on. You could see she didn't know what she should do with the box, it was an awkward size, and it didn't seem respectful just to put it on the ground. I didn't think that she'd be back after the crem and I was right.

She said, "What was she like? I didn't know her. I was just a child." Her eyes ached with all the holding back of tears. It took a lot for her to ask me, after everything that Fr John had said.

"She talked about you," I said at last. "She kept your letter."

That afternoon I went down to the shore and threw the earrings in the sea. They must have finished at the crematorium. The tide was coming in, the thick waves sliding fast across the Bay, and once I thought I saw the rubies catch the light, a glint of fire in the sand. Then they disappeared and it was far too late to bend and rescue them.

Two Wakes

By Kirsty Logan

' *Wake Week' or 'Fair Fortnight' began in the 19th century, when Glasgow factories and shipyards closed for a week at the end of July for workers' holidays. The north-west coast of England was a popular destination. The closure of shipyards and factories and standardization of the work week ended this tradition, though a ghost of it exists in Glasgow Fair weekend, a long weekend before the third Monday of July.*

1

Margot wasn't afraid. She wouldn't let the fortune-teller think that she was. She kept her face flat and emotionless as she examined the objects one by one. A sea box, the fortune-teller had called it, and although Margot had heard it at first as a *see box* – have a look-see, wait and see, let's just see about that – she realised now that everything inside it looked sea-beaten, sand-whacked, like it had emerged from a storm.

"You must touch them," said the fortune-teller. "One by one. Hold the charms. Let them feel your energy. Let them be a part of you."

Nonsense, thought Margot, sheer stuff and piffle. But still. It wasn't so bad to touch them. The starfish felt cool, its uneven bumps soothing on her fingertips. She wanted to raise it to her eye and peer into the hole at the centre, but when she lifted it to her face the faint smell of stale seawater from it made her insides lurch. She still felt the swoop in her belly, the burr and sway. The ferris wheel was right behind the fortune-teller's gauzy, overheated tent – was, in fact, the reason she'd come into the tent in the first place – and she knew that if she were to get up and twitch back the curtain, she'd see the turn of the wheel, its inevitability, its dizzying. But she wouldn't do that.

She put down the starfish and picked up a scratched brass compass. She expected it to be cool, but it was warm, as if it still held the body heat from the last person to touch it. She lingered on the mirror, with its shell-stuck frame, though she was careful to tilt it away so she couldn't see her reflection; she knew her sleepless nights showed beneath her eyes, and didn't want to be reminded. The finger-length key and the message in the bottle she picked up and cast aside quickly, eager now to get on with things. She ran her thumb over the clatter of golden coins, letting their indentations catch her rough fingerprints. She stacked them back into the box in a neat column, and the sea box was full again.

The fortune-teller closed the lid. "You are ready to hear your future?"

She smiled and shook back her hair; she had lipstick on her teeth and her hoop earrings were tangled in her curls. Margot was sure it must be a wig; how could she get it so huge and dark and shining? It seemed to swallow up all the light in the room – though it wasn't a room, was it? Just a collection of ratty shawls draped over some tent poles. It all meant nothing. This woman could tell her nothing.

Margot wasn't afraid. She wouldn't let herself be afraid. She picked up the sea box and shook it, cascading its contents across the table. Both women watched the objects tumble and settle.

"You are the centre," said the fortune-teller. "The objects closest to you are the most timely."

"Will they tell you about events that will happen soon?" said Margot. The starfish was so close it was almost touching her fingers. She pulled back, the salty smell catching in her throat.

"Perhaps. Or perhaps they symbolise events most important to you."

"And what about the objects further away?" Margot motioned to the key, the coins. She'd wanted them to mean something to her future; they seemed safe, strong. A key meant a house, coins meant money; these things inextricably linked and connected to steady ground, not the shifting sea. Nothing that had ever lived.

"As the charms radiate out, they symbolise events further in your future."

A future steadiness. Margot could accept that.

"Or," went on the fortune-teller, "they might not come at all. It depends."

"On what?"

"On your choices. There is no inescapable fate, only possibilities."

Without realising, Margot had reached for the starfish. She snatched her hand back.

"Touch it," said the fortune-teller.

"I don't want to."

"Yes." The fortune-teller smiled. "Pick it up."

Margot did. It was cool and bumpy, just as before. She waited, but nothing happened. "I don't understand."

"Shake it."

Margot did. She felt, rather than heard, a rattle from inside the starfish. She lifted it to her eye and looked into the hole at the centre. She rattled it again. Caught inside was a tiny shell. Margot couldn't help it: despite her sickness, despite her disbelief, she smiled. How small the shell looked in there. How safe.

"It is protected," said the fortune-teller, "until it wants to come out."

"And then what?"

"And then..." The fortune-teller raised her hands, palm-up. "Then there are possibilities."

The fortune-teller smiled wider, and she was beautiful then, her hair glossy and true, and Margot felt her smile drop as the world rose up in her.

"But what –"

But the world was rising indeed, right up her throat, and Margot spilled out of the fortune-teller's tent and onto her knees on the ground, breathing hard, swallowing bile, and she would not make a shaming mess in the middle of the fair with everyone around. What was she thinking, coming here? What had she hoped to learn? Pretending she needed a holiday, off to the seaside like any normal person. The truth was that she'd thought it would help to cross a border, even an arbitrary one between countries. Symbolic somehow, like it meant something. Ach, she was a bampot, right enough.

She knelt there alone in the dirt and met no one's eye and breathed hard and lost herself in memory until she was ready to go back inside and pay the fortune-teller for having told her the exact thing she didn't want to know.

Margot wasn't afraid. She'd heard stories – all women have heard stories – but she would be fine. The doctors knew what they were doing, didn't they? And the nurses' uniforms were so white, blinding really. Pressed and pristine. Surely nothing could go wrong in a place like this. But her watermelon belly, and the watery blood, and the waves of pain the pain oh god the pain the grit of her teeth so they creaked and seemed they'd break and it felt like all the bones between her ribs and knees were shattering splintering and how could a body feel like this and still be alive and here came another another breathe through it's okay steam-train breathing teeth clenched it's okay it's okay.

And she was back, she could open her eyes, the pain ebbed. The taste of salt in her mouth and she'd bitten her lip, torn off a flap of dry skin, beading red beneath. It was only recently that her lips had begun to crack, her skin too, everything leached out of her, tiny folded wrinkles at the corners of her eyes and mouth. She used to have pretty lips, petal-velvet. All the boys wanted to kiss them and she'd let them, some of them, the ones she liked. The one she'd liked the best she'd married, and that's how you get in these pickles really, isn't it? The nurses had called him and he was coming, he said he'd be here, and Margot just wanted him to be here before the baby. In fact if he could be here and she not here and still the baby here, that would be fine with her. She smiled against the swelling pain, her lip splitting again, and it was coming it was coming worse worse how could it be like this, how could anyone survive it, and she wouldn't scream she couldn't scream, her fists furled red urchins, her teeth creaking ship's boards in a storm, her spine a shattering mast, just breathe Margot just breathe through it Margot what would your mother say her cool hand on your forehead just breathe Margot my girl my lass my bonny just breathe, it's okay it's okay it's all going to be

But it wasn't okay.

There are possibilities.

Some of them are bad.

And we should be afraid of them.

Margot told herself that the barrier was not too flimsy, and it definitely did not remind her of a tin opener. She told herself that the carriage was not swaying, and even if it was it could not possibly sway upside down and tip her out. She told herself that she'd watched the ferris wheel go around and around and around, lifting children and women and men to the sky and back, and not a one of them had fallen out. It was okay. There were always possibilities, but usually one is most likely. Still, that didn't mean she had to open her eyes, did it?

Even here in her own darkness she could feel the swoop and spin of the wheel underneath her. Or not underneath her; around her. It moved with her, she moved with it. She was a part of it. The way it displaced air, the almost smell of it, the creak and swish, the clang. She was a part of that too. They moved together; she was inside it and it would keep her safe.

Margot wasn't afraid. She opened her eyes. The sky was blue, blue, endless, cotton-puff clouds and around that bluer than any sea. The barrier held her. The floor held her. Another baby was coming and she held it and she would keep holding it until she didn't need to any more. It had gone wrong before, but it was going to go right now.

There are possibilities, and just because one happens that doesn't mean it will happen again.

Margot stood and spread her arms wide. The carriage swayed but did not tip her out. Her feet felt steady on the unsteady floor. The wheel turned, the wind lifted her hair, the sun warmed her face. She was lifted into the sky, into the sun. She let herself be afraid, and it was okay.

2

The sun on his face. The sea air. Everyone he loves crammed on two benches on the seafront, him with a wean dripping ice-cream on each knee. He only gets one week away from the shipyards a year –

(*the crane looming over the brick-rowed houses, the clang and the clank so loud he could hear it in his dreams, the constant ache in his eardrums, the pressure of it in his throat, the constant pressure the pushing the groaning the need to cough to shout to scream*)

but it isn't so bad to be here really. George would have happily motored up and down the Clyde in a dinghy or soaked up the odd flash of sun in his deckchair in the garden, but the kids wanted a trip. Margot poring over the map, reading the names like they were poems: Ravenglass, Saltcoats, Buttermere,

Seascale, Whitehaven, Backbarrow. But it was the sea they wanted, so Margot chose Cleveleys. Fair enough. None of it's so bad: the train journey, the funfair, the seafront hotel. It's the least he can do for the kids really, as long as they enjoy it –

(he'd always worried that he wasn't giving them enough, his wife gone so quick and Margot the youngest only eighteen months, the girls had to step in with the housework so he could work all the hours God sent and it wasn't fair on them, was it, just kids they were, he'd tried so hard in those days to be two parents in one)

or at least the grandkids do. Too titchy to really know what's what, so they are, but still. Nice that they're all so close in age, and four of them too, no odd numbers making anyone feel left out. He doesn't even mind the money. No pockets in a shroud so there's no point, is there, in keeping your wallet shut so tight that when you finally open it, moths come barrelling out. Anyway, this bit's free, isn't it? The sun, the sea, the weans on his knee.

"Listen to this, Dad." Margot has got the paper spread across her knees and she's reading an advert, a full-page thing. "No longer need we envy the privileged few who can visit the historic battlefields of France and Belgium. A visit to the Scenic Railway permits us for a very reasonable sum to be a part of history."

George couldn't help letting out a snort then. "History it might be, but –

(envy they've put, bloody envy, what a cheek, he's a mind to rip this bench from its roots and throw it across the sand, get a bit of blood going, sever some limbs, crack some heads, maybe then they'd see it wasn't all bloody funfairs and ice-creams, that these cheap thrills were bought dear)

– we'll all be a part of history one day. Me and you and all of us."

"Don't be a grump, Dad. It says: Wounded soldiers who took part in the fighting in and around Yip-ress – Yup-res – Yeep? Anyway, it's the soldiers come up with it – conceived the idea

79

of constructing a full sized reproduction of the Trenches, with Dug-outs, Trench Hospitals, and Dressing Stations. We are further permitted to examine the trench mortars, periscopes and the "plum puddings" the enemy so disliked; also a variety of bombs; specimens of German helmets and weapons; unexploded shells and anti-aircraft guns are all –"

"Aye, all right, Margot. I get the point, you don't have to –

(*aye, he says to her, aye like it's nothing, as if it wasn't bad enough that he'd not just lived through two wars, but fought in the bastards too, and now what was it? a bloody funfair ride, like it was all just a bit of a laugh, don't know they're born these spoilt milk-fed little*)

read the whole bloody advert."

"It says it's as instructive as it is entertaining. It's got Second World War stuff too. Normandy, Tripoli, Hong Kong."

Suddenly the sun on George's face burns hotter. "What about Japan?"

Margot scans the advert. "It doesn't say. Why? Dad, are you listening? I asked you why. Is that where you were stationed?"

"Right, wee ones," says George, getting to his feet so the sugar-sticky weans scatter, "it's time we were offski, let's get you on that ferris wheel so I can –

(*Japan it was and Japan he wishes it was still, he never felt as happy as in those days, and you weren't supposed to say it, wartime is a bad time, a sad time, you're not meant to long for it but he did, and for her too, and the wean he was sure he'd left her with though she'd never said, never a reply to any of his letters though he'd tried, once a week then once a month then tapering to nothing but you couldn't blame him, could you, no wife now and four kids and couldn't be spending all his bloody nights writing bloody letters that she never bloody replied to*)

get a shot on the railway."

George has never been on a model railway before, so he doesn't know if they're all the same. With this one, he sits in a metal car the size of two large arses, which is fine for George as he has only one and it's medium-sized. A bar comes down over his knees and the car judders on. The backs of the cars are high so he can't see the people in front or behind, and George likes that. Nice to enjoy something in peace. He can hear the squeals and squabbles of the weans in the car in front, and he finds it –

(*bloody awful, what a bloody racket, didn't they have any respect? He'd raised his kids right so why were they raising their own kids so wrong, he just couldn't understand it, Sachiko wouldn't have raised her wean that way he was sure, and what would he say when he met the wee one? Would it know its daddy? He felt sick to think of it, but perhaps in a good way, sick with excitement*)

oddly soothing.

On the car goes, the car ca-clunking on the tracks, taking him through a succession of miniature scenes, a quarter the size of real things but the floor angled up like a theatre audience so he can see everything and it all looks real and good.

A trip round the world, things you wanted to see and also some things George would have said no-one would ever want to see, but here it all is, so what does he know? Battlefields it goes through, right enough, and he'd happily shut his eyes at that bit –

(*bloody disgusting, making death an attraction, they didn't have a clue what he and the boys had gone through, those little popping bombs and whiffs of smoke, bloody ridiculous, how would that wee thing ever rip off your leg or imbed a bloody great bit of shrapnel in your eye? He'd seen that and more, and now he was meant to sit on a bloody train behind a bloody safety bar and pretend there was ever such a thing as safety*)

but that's not what he wants. The battlefields are only one part of the model railway.

There's Hollywood, all big lit-up letters taller than a man. Smiling models of glamorous girls from the pictures, their dresses fluttering over hot air vents, teasing but not showing.

Lights that catch in your eyes so you can't blink them out. Men looking dapper, their hair smooth and neat like George used to have his back when –

(and bloody hell, he should sort that, would it work to lick his palm and smooth it down? His hair was grey now, the texture changed, not sleek like it was but wiry and unruly, an old man's hair to go with his old man's face, and would Sachiko recognise him like this? Would she still want him?)

he was serving.

And then, finally, comes Japan. The sumo men with their bellies round as the moon. The white flag with its red spot like a drop of blood. And of course, the white-faced geishas in their kimonos, but that's not what catches his eye. One miniature scene is an alley of trees, pink cherry blossoms puffed up on their trunks like candy floss, with people meandering beneath. And there she is, right at the back, walking alone under a paper parasol. Everything is the same as he remembers: her black dress with the ruffled sleeves, her floppy hat with the satin band, her little white shoes. He can even smell her perfume.

George is so entranced he doesn't even blink, which is how he knows he isn't imagining it when she smiles and tilts her head at him. But the car judders on, and the bar presses tight over his legs, and when he tries to call her name all that comes out is a muffled wheeze, and over the sound of it he knows he hears her calling to him.

He goes around again, and once more he smells her perfume, and once more she smiles at him.

He goes around again. And again.

On his last time around, George pouches out his belly as the attendant comes round to check the bar is pressed down tight –

(he'd kept trim, porridge made with water and served in a shallow sea of skimmed milk for breakfast, puddings only on Saturdays, shoveled the snow from his own steps every year, so it was hard for him to pretend he'd let himself go to fat, even

though it was for a good cause, it was worth it, never matter what some ride attendant thought of him anyway)

so that when he relaxes back, there's a good bit of wiggle room between him and the bar. The weans have long given up, bored after one trip, and disappeared off for a shot on something flashier and spinnier and noisier.

George sits back in the car and waits. The battlefields. The popping bombs, the smoke. The blinking, blinding Hollywood lights. The coy geishas. And then, finally, the pink trees and the woman with the parasol. She smiles and tilts her head at him again – but it's different this time, her smile questioning. An invitation. A question unanswered.

George steps out of the model railway car and into the avenue of cherry blossoms. The breeze lifts his brown hair, his rough uniform feeling good and true against his wrists. His leg muscles stretch strong and long as he walks towards Sachiko.

She turns to him, breathing his name, and her eyes are bright and her smile is wide, and he opens his arms ready for her, and he walks away from his past and into his future.

Mono No Aware

By Lucy Wilkinson Yates

My Aunt Leonor is skinny and tall and even though she stopped smoking many years ago, she still holds her fingers with a little gap where the cigarette should fit, jammed right up to the knuckle. She spent many of her younger years working for a big company in Japan where, on account of her height and ferocity, she was very efficient at selling photocopiers to companies who didn't need them. She came home a couple of years ago. Things have been different since then. The Longridge cousins say she had a Japanese wife, that Leonor changed when she left. The photograph on her mantelpiece says they could be right. Mum says not.

It takes us an hour to get Leonor out of her flat and into the car, what with her checking and the way that we, by our mere presence, upset her routine. You can see the sadness in her eyes when she realises that she has to start again, like being sent to Monopoly prison. She stamps her feet on the doormat, counts her breaths as though they measure out some unseen force that has the power to burn down the house if she breathes incorrectly. She counts the turns of the key and the rattles of the doorknob. Even when she gets the numbers right, it has to *feel* right. It's difficult to imagine a person concentrating harder.

But now we're in the car and on our way. From the front seat, she says what we are all thinking:

"They wouldn't recognise Blackpool now."

Outside, the privet hedges of the suburbs grow slowly higher and wilder as we drive out of town, our own town, which is not Blackpool. This used to be a bad thing but is now, I think, good. My grandparents loved Blackpool, because it was a feeling as well as a place. For them, happiness was mapped out like a songline that passed through the Winter Gardens and ended with the wooden forks at the seafront chippy. I wonder what Aunt Leonor's Japanese wife would think of Blackpool, of the palm-readers and 99s and waxworks. From the way she looks, I can tell that Aunt Leonor is wondering the same thing. Her eyes shine like the illuminations before switching off abruptly. We all look out of the windows because we don't know what to say on a day like this. Leonor breaks the silence.

"It was classy back then. The Americans always wanted to go." The Americans were our cousins in America, the product of an aunt who emigrated to marry a GI after the war. She raised a flock of babies and taught them all to speak with Lancashire accents until they went to school and learnt better.

In the back with me and Dan, my mother smiles. On her lap is a carrier bag, and she pats it contentedly. "It *was* a classy place," she says. "She loved taking the Americans."

"And she loved – "

"Lewis's."

"I was going to say the pier," says Leonor. "The penny machines."

"Those too."

My father is driving, and you can tell that he is trying to be solemn for the occasion. He has one of those faces that makes babies laugh and adults feel contented, although right now he is doing his best to hold it steady and straight. In the rear view mirror, you can see the muscles tense and relax under his pink skin. His laugh is my favourite thing about him, because he does it to make other people feel good. He doesn't laugh today though. He turns on the radio, flicks through the stations and turns it off again before craning his neck to see us in the rear-view mirror. We must look nervous. We're wearing the most sombre workout clothes we own, and my brother has his hood pulled up. It barely covers his head; the rim puckers where the cord is pulled tight. He is quieter than I've ever seen him. He's still at an age where he hates things, but today he just looks uncomfortable.

"It's not illegal," says my dad, glancing back at us. "I've looked it up."

"On the You Tube," says Mum. *The You Tube* showed them how to mix the ashes, which they did in the garden on a non-windy day as the vlogger had recommended. "We used a new trowel though," she adds. "Out of respect."

"They didn't put that in the video," says Dad.

"No," says Mum. "They didn't."

Aunt Leonor wiggles her fingers like she is ashing a cigarette, and leans her elbow on the lip of the window. She looks out and gazes far further than the hedgerows and shop-fronts that the rest of us see. I wonder if she is thinking about her Japanese woman. She ashes her invisible cigarette more vigorously. Leonor ashes her cigarette in a special way that I think is part of her checking. She taps each finger on the length of the cigarette in order like this: index, middle, ring, little. She does this four times with each hand and then, if the cigarette was real, she would take a drag. As she gave up smoking many years ago, she raises her fingers to her mouth and sighs instead.

We drive past an old, half-timbered house that my parents almost bought when I was a baby. There are no hedges; it seems almost obscene. As we pass, my dad usually tells the story about how it has a moat (he's always wanted a moat), and then my mum tells us that it would have been a ridiculous place to live, because of both the moat and the ghosts. She's not superstitious, but she doesn't believe in tempting fate. They don't tell the story today. Mum holds tighter to the bag of ashes as we go around the sharp corner, where you can just see the moat from the road.

The lanes between the edge of town and the first slopes of Beacon Fell are crooked and strange. You think you're going one way and you get lost; you get lost and then end up where you were aiming for in the first place. Mum says that the young farmers mix up the road signs for fun. My aunt solemnly agrees. She says she caught them once when she was out in the motor-car with the Longridge cousins. The hedgerows are high and every so often studded with over-ripe blackberries that stain the road purple where they fall. Three cars pass us going in the opposite direction, but it's too late to be the morning rush. If there even is a morning rush out here. We set off at a carefully chosen time, late enough to miss the commuter traffic but early enough that the daytrippers wouldn't have arrived yet.

My grandparents – for my grandparents are in the bag on my mother's lap – were vocal enough about their plans for the great ever after. My dad always says that they were forward-thinking for Catholics. It's we who have been indecisive. They'd lived through enough war and forgetting and emigration that they didn't want graves. They wanted to be scattered on a hill, or at least a natural feature of some kind. Something that their descendants could tip their hats to, rather than clean. As ideas go, it's either humble or gently megalomaniac, depending on how you look at it. During one of their weekly phone calls, mum and Leonor had discussed where to scatter them. They thought about Blackpool, but decided that there wouldn't be much space for eternal rest in between all of the arcades and burger bars, and that the idea of children building sandcastles out of ashes was mildly disturbing "although quite sweet," as Leonor later said.

Gran had been a widow for two decades when she died. Mum and Leonor chose the place a few months after that; it took us another decade to decide upon the date what with me moving away for university and Leonor moving back and making a prison for herself among the packing-boxes.

As the car climbs slowly through the wooded slopes of the fell, everyone is quiet. You can hear the gearbox shifting as the slope gets steeper. Leonor moves her invisible cigarette into her right hand and curls her body in close around it, folding in her arms and legs and shoulders until her right hand, palm up and fingers out, stands out like the end of a ball of wool. It's beautiful here. You can see Lancashire unfolding below, from the green fringes of the fell, to our town and finally out across the Fylde to the grey, flat sea.

"In Japanese, there's a phrase," says Aunt Leonor, pausing to mark the transition from English. Her voice shifts slightly as though moving into another key. "*Mono no aware.* The –"

"The gentle sadness of things," says Dan, sitting forward and re-tying his hood strings so that only the very centre of his face is exposed. "We know."

"How did you know that?" asks Leonor, turning to look at the three of us crammed into the back seat.

"Because you say it *every time* we're quiet," he says. "Like there's something sad about being quiet."

"Shut up," I say to Dan, because I can't think of a better way to remind him about the ways Leonor tends to fill up silence. I see my mother, in between the two of us, wonder whether it would be right to tell us off with the ashes on her knee, but her wondering is cut short by my father pulling off the road and onto the empty car park. There are no families here yet. We all feel relieved.

"Here," he says. "Wasn't it?"

We walk down the slope, where the ground is all muddy with summer rain and other people's shoes. Dad goes first to check the footing and mum goes next, carrying my grandparents like a packed lunch in the carrier bag. Leonor is next, since she's too well-dressed to be inconspicuous. Me and Dan walk at the back, him in his outgrown hoodie and me in leggings. We go over the stile at the bottom of the field. When mum hands over the bag of ashes as she climbs up, Leonor's hand trembles. She looks relieved when she can hand it back, and taps furiously for a few minutes. She does it inside her pockets where she thinks we can't see.

Over the stile is the place they have chosen, a field that is thick with grass and sloped just perfectly so that you can lie down and look out over the countryside before you. I haven't been here before, but it seems like a good place for the two of them to spend eternity. You can see the spires of our town and in the distance, the neat cut of the shore where the grey smudge of Blackpool ceases. I wonder if it really has changed since my grandparents used to go, or whether it's we who are different. We stand in a line looking at the view.

"This'll do for me, when the time comes," says Leonor, still tapping in her pocket. She looks at us all and says, as though she wants to be sure we've heard, "You can put me here too."

We stand a moment in silence, unsure whether to make a ceremony up on the spot. Leonor quietly sings The Lord is My Shepherd, which seems appropriate since we are in a field. My mother says a short prayer and then gets the trowel out as we all say Amen. It shines as if it's been polished for the occasion. Mum demonstrates the technique she's seen on the You Tube, digging the trowel deep into the carrier bag and scattering the ashes wide across the grass like chicken feed. The finer parts rise up with the wind and make shadows before settling. We take turns like this: first Mum, then Dad. Dan looks pale before taking his turn. He holds his shoulders wide and takes his hood down out of respect. I wonder if this makes him feel more like a grown-up or less. I feel like a child as tears prick my eyes. It feels wrong to be scattering them like this, like grass seed. I take a half-trowel of them and imagine for a moment that we could keep them on the mantelpiece instead. Silence falls and they all look at me, looking at the little bit of my grandparents on the trowel.

Leonor puts her arm around my shoulders and says, extending her cigarette fingers to the west: "Scatter a bit over there, love. So they can see Blackpool."

Blackpool Lights

By Anita Sethi

The lights flicker along the pier and the sea is thick and slick, spread out as far as the eye can see. The surface of the sea gleams like freshly brushed black hair covering the earth, as wavy as Sohni's hair. The lights dance in the darkness, sometimes slowly, sometimes in a hectic motion. There is a lit-up tram, inching along in the night, a ship, a crown, dancing people. We're stuck in the huge snake of traffic, inching through the lights. This is our closest sea, the nearest world's edge we have.

Dad leaves me and Sohni on our own while he goes on the grown-up rides with Ash; the Big Dipper and the Avalanche. They hurry off into the queues and are soon lost amongst the anonymous crowds. Me and Sohni wait beside the great clown which sits in the middle of the Pleasure Beach, sealed behind a large glass casing. He has huge laughing lips, and sits rocking back and forth, back and forth, his body catching neon yellow light and throwing it into our eyes like swords. Every now and then between his cartoonish, dayglo laughs he crumples into tears, and then jerks back into his roaring, mesmerising, rocking happiness.

We stand watching the clown, our hands clutching two purple plastic Catherine Wheels stuck on sticks, which revolve slowly round and round, round and round in the wind. Sohni reaches out to stroke my hair but I instinctively jerk away. Wherever I look, the clown seems to follow me around after that, like the kind of visual echoes you get after looking directly into too bright a light; tiny flashes haunting your eyeballs.

When Dad and Ash return from the rides, their expressions mirror each other – a wild, emptied-out, distant look in their shining eyes, as if the motion of plunging through space has ripped right through to the quick of them.

We all go into the Black Hole ride, queuing up in the long line, beside graffiti tippexed into the peeling painted railings – "This is our last night"; "Here comes our death". The queue inches forward, further towards the Black Hole, edging us closer to the darkness. Then we are stepping into a carriage which clangs shut and we whoosh away. Soon, it is so pitch black that you can't see your own body, you can't tell how high up you are, how steep the drop is, how far you are going to plummet into the darkness. Everything has been given up to the darkness, except for a scattering of blue pinpricks – not just above, but all around, adding to the sense of spacelessness, skewing your sense of your own bodily self, which loses its contours as the blackness drinks you up. You grapple to keep a hold of yourself but then let yourself go, dissolve, a bit like struggling not to fall asleep, trying to hold onto your consciousness, stop yourself falling.

But then I am falling, falling, falling through the darkness, plunging through the pitch-black at rapid speed and I feel a surge of fear in my belly, as if there is a black hole within me, as well as without. Then I am shooting sideways, upwards, across, yet always it seems as if I am in one and the same position – blackness. I close my eyes and there is the same endless dark matter. Is this what it would be like to travel through outer space? For it to be so dark that it's impossible to see your companions in the journey let alone your own self? At first I'm terrified of the interminable hole but after a few moments I let go of the fear and relish swooping and diving around in the vast dark space, with no contours or delineations, no boundaries visible at all.

Then the light floods back, a glare of electric, and we are spat out of the darkness and the emptiness as the carriage wheels shriek to a halt. From blackness we make our way towards colour. In the Funhouse, huge slides spill down into bright red and green and yellow little plastic worlds. One slide is near-vertical.

"I dare you to go on it", says Ash to me and Sohni but I don't dare, and they don't care that I don't dare as off they go, and I watch from below as Ash and Sohni walk high up, disappearing amidst the throng. I watch people plunge down and crash into the colours and then return to the top again and smash down once more – as if something is ripped out of them in the process, each time, by the violence of smashing into the colours, something inside is purged. I don't join them, too scared, always, of falling, of my body becoming unstuck from the surface of the slide and tumbling through the air with nothing to hold it.

The Funhouse spills into the hall of mirrors and the hall of mirrors into the Haunted House – or is the hall of mirrors part of the haunted house? Sohni smashes into herself walking through air that isn't air but glass, and I slip up as I look down and see myself swimming all over the floor.

Outside again, I catch a glimpse of myself reflected in the clown's glass cage. I too have that weird, emptied-out, look of the wilderness in my eyes.

The Big Wheel is glimmering, its circle of lights flickering in the blackness, the lighted circle slowly revolving.

"How's your Mum?" asks Dad, the pupils of his eyes drawing me again into the Black Hole ride.

"Fine," I say.

"How's school?" asks Dad, his eyes then tracing the circular pattern of the lighted wheel.

"Fine," I say.

"Be nice to your Mum, OK," says Dad.

"OK," I say, looking for his proper eyes but not able to see them clearly now, only able to see the revolving wheel filling his black pupils up with fire.

We wind our way back past the black wavy hair, which is streaked with silver now, and patches of gleaming white, as the moon has risen up above it – full and heavy. The lure of the sea calls. Far, far out, the huge loneliness threatens.

Me and Sohni race along the beach, running along the open expanse, and the wind bites into my flesh. I hear my heart beating, and feel alive and free.

"Don't go too far out," Dad shouts after us, his voice sounding echoey and fading the further we run, but we keep on running.

"We venture right up to the shining hair and then, down on hands and knees, not minding at all about our trousers getting wet and cold, reach out to stroke that wave. We watch the silver vanish as soon as we touch it, and feel the cold slimy water and scream as our hands brush against litter floating in the sea. I stroke the water, and now the thick black hair is parting and a bright image is surfacing through the blackness. Me and Mum running through summer waves, Sohni with a bucket in her hands, looking for shells. Mum carrying me in her arms, me held tight against her warm wet body, held safely away from the sea, which I was scared even to touch, then. Scared of its huge emptiness, the way it went on and on and you couldn't see where it ended. A 'horizon' they called it at school. "Set your sights on the horizon," the teacher said.

Then the memory shimmers, the five brown bodies lose their solidity, sinking back down below the surface, the moonlight settling again on the water, covering up the bodies. I feel a sharp *thwack* on my arm then and the memory vanishes completely as I turn to see Ash is throwing things as he walks towards us.

94

"Stop throwing them at me!" I yell.

"I'm throwing them at the sea," he insists, walking closer and in his hand I see a pile of pebbles and shells. I stoop down and rummage around for shells then, feeling about in the sand until my palm curves around a big one, and as Dad's voice floats louder and louder across to us – "Time to go home now" – I pocket the shell.

I try and try to retrieve the images that surfaced through the black waves. I try to retrieve them all the way back to Manchester. As we slip down the gleaming snaky near-empty motorway and bickering starts up between us, I try to stop the images from drowning within me, I try to cling on to the patch of bright red that is Sohni running towards me, I try to cling on to the imprint of Mum's arms around me, the smell of the day, the feeling of safety, but it is all drowning now, sinking away as screaming starts up in the car, Sohni yelling to Dad about how our brother was throwing pebbles at us, him shouting back to shut up and stop lying, and Dad's voice silent, the silence echoing so loudly. From the back seat, I look up into the rear-view mirror and can see Dad's eyes, fixed ahead on the road, and they seem to be glistening with tears.

When the car halts at a service station, the images of that day of togetherness have all but drowned – I can no longer summon the expressions on those five faces, I can no longer recall the happiness in mum's eyes. "I'm scared of going back to the haunted house," whispers Sohni, which is how we've begun to talk about our home. By the time the car arrives outside our front door, it is all drowned. I can no longer recall the feel of Mum's arm around me, the warmth of her salty skin.

Dad delivers us back to the haunted house and when he sees that we have opened the door, he speeds off into the rain-choked air.

Mum is curled up sleeping on the sofa. Her loud snoring breaks us all open into shuddering laughs, rocking laughs, which then somersault into breathless, helpless sobbing, and then back into the laughs. None of these sounds stops Mum's snoring. As I cry-laugh I think of the clown. That clown continues to follow me around, haunting me. The clown's face doesn't fade and finally disappear over the following days; instead, it grows, popping up in the corner of the classroom, swimming in the sauce of my chicken curry, leering out of the heavy grey clouds.

"If you hold it to your ear, you will hear the sea caught in there forever," Mum tells me one day when I show her the big shell I brought back with me, the shell all smooth after being bruised and tossed by the sea's rage.

I think Mum must be going mad and don't believe her, but then she gently puts the shell on my ear and tells me to be very quiet and hold my breath in. I listen more carefully than I have ever listened before. Then I hear it, the sound tickling my ears and making me laugh. The sound of the sea washes through my mind, as if there is a whole world caught inside the small shell.

"Will the sea be in there forever?"

"Forever. It will always be with you and never disappear. So you better keep this shell safe."

I hold on to the shell, feel its smooth, solid, pale pink body, and inspect the tiny lines fanning out and the marble swirls on it. I press it to my ear and can hear the sea's raging and crashing, the song of the sea, and the sound of the wind, and know there is a world outside of these walls, a world elsewhere.

Every day I listen to its secret song and remember how wide the horizons can be.

Katy

By Andrew Michael Hurley

He hated this fucking place and Saturday nights were the worst. All high heels and terrace chants. It was only just after six but there were girls already weak-ankled with drink, crying and vomiting in doorways. In one street he'd seen a man being strong-armed into the back of a police van and then around the corner in the next a fight had spilled out of a karaoke bar as he stopped a homeless woman to show her Katy's photograph. She hadn't been able to hear him properly over the shouting and the music and went off with her dog before he could ask her to look again.

A carnival, thought David. That was all life was for these people. A pageant of drums, sequins and flesh. He watched two women in devil costumes arguing outside a betting shop and made his way down to the promenade.

The Illuminations still had another week to run and cars and coaches edged along the seafront under the swinging effigies of cartoon characters and butterflies. For a moment or two, he stood beneath the canopy of Harry Ramsden's trying to pick Katy out from the flow of hoods and umbrellas, then moved on past the Tower. The lights on the girdered legs rose into the drizzle and the top was lost in cloud that sat low along the coastline. Every window he passed was steamed. Every face was as damp as flannel. But even so, the pavements were packed from the shop doorways to the kerb. Katy had chosen a good night to lose herself.

David stopped a family coming out of the Wetherspoons and showed them the photograph on his phone. It had been taken a couple of years earlier when Katy was fourteen and although she had changed since then – she'd got taller and slimmer and grown her hair – there were still enough similarities in her eyes and her mouth for someone to recognise her.

The father, vacant, with the sour, stewed smell of someone who'd been drinking all day, ignored him and turned away to light a cigarette inside his coat. But the mother angled her head and looked closely as she rolled a pushchair back and forth to quieten the baby screaming behind the raincover.

"Is she yours?" she asked.

"Yes," said David.

"She been missing long?"

"A while," David said, thinking it would garner more sympathy than if he told her Katy had only been gone for an hour.

The mother looked again and with something syrupy and alcoholic on her breath, said, "shame, she's a pretty thing, isn't she?" and finally gave in to the tugging hands of her two little girls who wanted candy floss and glow-sticks from the stand on the street corner. The father put his cigarette between his lips and groped his pockets for change as he followed them unsteadily, one set of shoelaces untied.

A pretty thing, right enough. Out here tonight it would be impossible for her to be anonymous. Men would queue up to buy her drinks and she'd accept them all.

He'd searched in at least half a dozen pubs already, each of them happy and violent, full of men who laughed very loudly, men with bald heads and big bodies. And opening the door the family had emerged from, he now worked his way between the tables of The Albert showing the photograph to those he thought might care. After the last shake of the head he went back onto the promenade where the wind filled the bowl of his umbrella and turned it inside out.

He still couldn't quite understand how Katy had done it. As far as he knew, the locks on the car doors were impervious to any tampering. But she was a clever girl. He didn't doubt that she'd been planning the whole thing ever since they'd told her that they were taking her to see Mrs Yarrow again.

She'd bided her time and when David had stopped at the pedestrian crossing by Ma Kelly's she'd opened the back door and lost herself in the crowds on Topping Street. Janet had gone after her but come back to where David had parked the car a few minutes later in despair. Rummaging in the back seat for an umbrella, she was determined to go searching, but David had persuaded her to take the car and go home in case Katy went back there. He would call when he'd found her. She couldn't have gone far.

At the time Janet had reluctantly agreed and driven away down Talbot Road but worry had clearly got the better of her and the screen of David's mobile was filled with text messages. *Coral Island?* the most recent. It was a possibility. Whenever they happened to drive past there, Katy had always begged to go inside.

The place was thick with the smell of fried food and burnt sugar, but David was glad to be somewhere warm and dry and edged from one glowing machine to the next, excusing himself, showing the photograph. The older ones – the men in zip-up cardigans, the trunk-legged women on mobility scooters – took the time to look and pity but the teenagers yanking at steering wheels or squinting down the sights of plastic machine guns ignored him as if he were a beggar with a cardboard cup. The younger kids, running their hands surreptitiously along the troughs of the one-armed bandits for forgotten winnings, thought he was someone in authority and scattered.

With so many people there and every bell and buzzer declaring itself, voices and machines congealed into a vile discord.

He could hardly make himself heard at the change booth when he showed the photograph to the giantess behind the window, her bare forearms as thick and white as fish-bellies.

"Sorry," she said but seemed reluctant to pass the phone back through the coin tray. She asked if he was a policeman.

"I'm her father," said David.

The woman kept her eyes on him and then examined the photograph again.

"What was she wearing?" she said, testing him, David thought.

He described Katy's blue duffle coat, the denim shirt with the roses embroidered on the collar, jeans, white trainers. The woman, too big for the glass box, exhibited like a curio, leant on the counter and set her face as if to say she'd seen a dozen girls that evening who might have looked like that.

"Anything else?" she said.

He could have mentioned the way Katy sometimes stared through him, the strength she had in her, despite the slender frame. She'd knocked Mrs Yarrow to the floor more than once.

"Have you seen her or not?" David asked.

"There was a girl with some boys earlier," said the woman, nodding over David's shoulder into the twittering grove of fruit machines.

"And you think it was her?" said David and she shrugged.

"Maybe," she said, giving him back his phone. "Look, it's busy, you'll have to move," and David glanced at the queue that had grown behind him.

Having kept them all waiting, he didn't think they would be interested in helping him and so he put his phone away and went to search the corner the cashier had indicated. There were no boys, only solitary men, their faces lit by the flickering buttons, thumbing in coins and sipping pints from thin plastic beakers that buckled when they were gripped. None of them had seen Katy.

Back on the front, past the Sea Life Centre and Madame Tussauds and the horse-drawn Cinderella carriages, David looked in every one of the gift shops, squeezing between the people sheltering from the rain. Katy had little or no money of her own, but he knew that she would happily browse the tat, shaking the snowglobes, coveting the stacked batons of rock.

In the last place an elderly couple turned the rack of postcards and a loud hen party was trying on feather boas and plastic trilbys, but there was no Katy. Nor was she in any of the chippies or the 10p bingo halls. Beyond Foxhall Street there was nothing but hotels and the Lights, which ran on and on, brillianting in arches over the wet road. He didn't think Katy would have gone any further and to satisfy himself that he had exhausted all the places she might have hidden before he turned back, David made a final search up and down the aisles of Carousel, Happy Dayz and Slots-O-Fun and then crossed the tram tracks to Central Pier.

The wind met him face on. Blustery and brine-thick. The tide was coming in too. A growing, incessant wash that broke against the stanchions beneath. A few gulls appeared out of the darkness to pick through what had blown out of the bins, unchased and unhurried on this damp autumn night. The rain had passed over now and the planks reflected the wind-jigged lights that were festooned around the amusement booths. Katy wasn't at any of them. Not throwing darts for one of the giant white rabbits that hung suffocated in plastic bags above the boards. Not queuing for the ghost train.

It was getting late. She hadn't eaten since breakfast (Mrs Yarrow always insisted Katy came to her with an empty stomach) and chances were that her belly had started complaining and she was making her way home, drenched and sorry. Wherever she was, he hoped that she was alone. He hoped that no one had offered her a lift. For their sake.

David brought up the photograph on his phone again and moved from person to person and then stood by the waltzers trying to see if Katy was among the grinning, hair-whipped faces that lurched towards him and then retracted into the dim interior of the ride.

He realised that he'd caught the attention of the teenage boys who were smoking and drinking by the Victorian carousel. One of them knocked up his chin at David and mouthed something inaudible, and to make it seem as though he was there with a purpose other than to stare at young girls, David joined the queue for the coffee stand. The boys looked over at him and laughed but were soon distracted when one of them raised his can to the ferris wheel and cheered.

As the baskets swept upwards past the operator's booth, David spotted Katy sitting in one of them with a boy, his pals below goading him on to kiss her, to give her one. On the next revolution, he saw that he was chubby and acned and would have been easily flattered out of his money by a good-looking girl. They circled again and now the boy had his arm around Katy's shoulder, his elbow crooked at her neck.

David phoned Janet and she answered, relieved.

"Tell Mrs Yarrow I've found her," he said. "And then come with the car."

The ferris wheel slowed and came to a standstill, leaving Katy and the boy swinging high up. The boy planted a kiss on Katy's cheek and when he saw David standing there looking he gave a protective sneer and moved closer to her. He'd no doubt make a fuss when they got off the ride and Katy was taken away from him; he might even try to prove himself in front of his pals, not knowing that David was doing him a favour. Not knowing who he'd been riding the wheel with.

Katy would hopefully concede and come with him of her own accord. David didn't want to have to drag her into the car by her elbow like a child. She was sixteen now. But then, her complaints about Mrs Yarrow's house had never changed in the eight years they'd been taking her there. The place was cold, she said, and smelled of drains. The wooden stool she was made to sit on gave her splinters. And Mrs Yarrow always tried to hurt her.

That wasn't true at all. The treatment might have been painful, momentarily, but it was never deliberately brutal. The pressure Mrs Yarrow applied to Katy's head had to be strong otherwise nothing would happen.

It was the *thought* of the procedure that had made Katy open the car door and run off, that was all. She said herself that she always felt much better afterwards when she looked at what she'd brought up into the bowl on her lap, the blacker the better.

Time was, they'd have given her a lollipop to take away the taste and as a reward for being a good girl, but she was old enough now not to need incentives. She knew what would happen if she didn't see Mrs Yarrow. She knew that she had no choice.

Acceptance, said Mrs Yarrow, had been a path of sharp stones for all of them, but the only path. There was no cure. Not even time, which David and Janet had once trusted to right all Katy's wrongs. They'd firmly believed that her cruelty, even the spontaneous kind, was a phase; a surfacing of some primal urge for dominance that found its perfect host in the egoism of small children and naturally ebbed away again. And for a time they thought it had.

After the meetings in the headmaster's office, after the looks from other parents in the playground, after the appointments with doctors who hadn't helped her then and still couldn't now, they'd moved Katy to a different school and by the age of eight it seemed that she'd started to change. Although when her birthday came around in October and she asked if she could have some classmates over for a party, David and Janet had agreed with equal measures of delight and apprehension.

On the day itself, they'd hovered around the kitchen table while the girls ranked their teachers and spiked sausages with forks, and, uneasy about Katy finding one of the other girls alone in the quieter part of the garden behind the greenhouse, Janet had suggested a game of musical statues rather than Hide and Seek. They'd cut the cake with a plastic knife and made sure that the birthday girl won Pass the Parcel, but gradually they'd edged back and enjoyed watching Katy trying to teach her friends how to fly the octopus kite they'd bought her.

She'd seen it in one of the cheap shops on the prom and it was all she'd wanted – a life-sized facsimile of the real thing with rust-coloured tentacles and suspicious eyes. But the afternoon was cold and still and so it would not lift at all, no matter how much they all shouted encouragement and instructions. David told Katy she would have to wait. The wind would come back. Living by the sea, they could depend on it.

A few days later, a Sunday, they drove down the coast to Saint Anne's, where the grass on the dunes was wild and loud and loose sand blew in tongues across the road. The beach was empty but for a few private figures walking their dogs half a mile away at the white edge of the water, sending the knots and oystercatchers swarming. It was a good day for birdwatching, David told Katy. You could tell by the way the sea roared that the tide coming in was churning up plenty of food, betraying the crabs and the starfish. She was glad, she said, that her octopus could fly.

Katy dumped her boots and socks and ran across the pleated flats until she came to where she thought the wind was strongest, marking an X with her bare heel.

They spooled out the lines of the kite and when Janet threw it into the air, jumping herself with the effort, David showed Katy how to pull back on the plastic handles and keep the thing airborne. The wind quickly took it flapping and erratic, and on his knees behind her, his gloves over hers, David helped Katy bring it under control and then gently rotated her wrists in order to pay out the cords. Soon the octopus was high up under the clouds, its appendages fluttering like the tails of tadpoles. Katy looked over her shoulder at David and he knew that from her grin she was enjoying the way the force of the wind was being channelled down the strings and into her hands. How much stronger it was when it could blow unhindered in the upper air. Through the padding of her coat David felt her arms straining but she insisted he let go of her, which he did, and stood back to watch her working the lines. She dug her feet into the sand and for ten, fifteen, twenty minutes, she stared up at the kite, trying to keep it steady with little adjustments of pull and tug.

Eventually, Janet came over, rubbing her arms, putting her palms to Katy's cheeks to show how cold she was.

"Come on," she said. "Let's warm up somewhere."

Reining the kite back in was like dragging an anchor from deep water and it seemed to take an age before the octopus was close enough for them to see the detail on its skin and suckers. Buffed and kicked by the squalls that ricocheted between the dunes, the kite spun and then nose-dived into the sand and Katy raced off to recover it. The lines were twisted up and she set about turning the kite one way and then the other, chewing her bottom lip as she tried and failed to work out the puzzle.

It had been one of the times – and there had been others, he was sure – when David felt as though he could allow himself to love her.

The three of them had walked for half a mile and found a sheltered spot under a high dune. Katy went off with her bucket and spade to dig for the pink spire shells that she liked most of all and while David opened the thermos Janet set about untangling the lines of the kite.

They talked.

Kissed.

Listened to the grass and the birds.

It was an afternoon of normal things: tea, weather.

They watched a black raincloud coming off the sea like the blade of a plough and David turned and looked up at the top of the dune and called Katy's name.

"She won't come, you know," said Janet, standing up and fitting the kite into its plastic holder. "She'll be having too much fun."

Dusting off the sand from his backside, collecting Katy's little wellingtons and balled-up socks, David started labouring up the dune and Janet followed him to the windy crest.

Katy's trail was easy to pick up and the ridges held a record of her search for the best digging site. Her footprints would lead one way and then double back to strike off at a different angle. She'd gone much further than David had expected and when Janet took hold of his hand he reassured himself as much as her.

"It's not as if we won't find her, is it?" he said, indicating the footholes ahead. "When they end, that's where she'll be."

Even so, Janet started calling Katy's name.

The line of divots finally petered out where the marram grass grew thinly over a hummocking of bricks. There'd once been a café here, David seemed to remember, overcome since its demolition by the creeping dunes. Below was a hollow into which the sea had thrown a litter of bladder wrack and mussels, plastic nets and bright blue rope. It being such a fierce afternoon, it was likely that the next tide would reach so far as to take it all back.

David saw Katy first because she called to him and waved, but Janet, he realised, was distracted by something else. Directly below them at the foot of the steep cliff a man writhed slowly like an insect dying on a window ledge. A large clump of cement lay by a tartan rug, where a lunch box sat unopened and a pair of dropped binoculars looked away from what was happening.

Janet went down first, making apologies to the man over and over, but didn't want to go too near and knelt to watch him limply gouging a line in the sand with his foot. David found a different route and came into the hollow on his back when a chunk of sand gave way.

"Look, Daddy," said Katy and showed him the shells she'd collected, the little strawberry-coloured cornets and the ribbed eyelids of cockles.

She went back to excavating the hole she'd made and David looked over at the man. The back of his head and the back of his cagoule glistened.

Janet was crying loudly and David called to her, then again, and she got up and came over.

"Can you hold this, Mummy?" said Katy, handing her the bucket. "Did you untangle the kite?"

Janet stared at her and then nodded.

"Can we go and find starfish now?" Katy said. "I've never seen a starfish."

David managed to say something about the rain and the cold and the incoming tide and Katy smiled amicably as she put on the socks and boots that he passed to her.

Not looking behind them, not listening to the scuffing of the man's foot they went off through the debris to find a way out of the dunes, Katy talking about the kite and her birthday party and what she'd be doing at school the next morning.

When they were back on the beach, with the space to walk three abreast, she took hold of Janet's hand and then David's, gripping much too firmly for a girl of her age.

The ferris wheel turned in increments, bringing Katy and the boy to the ground. David went over and when she saw him waiting in the crowd the smile left her face. The boy looked at him and held Katy's hand.

"What do you want, mate?" he said.

David ignored him. "We need to go, Katy," he said. "Say goodbye to your friends now."

The other boys started to form a circle around him. The tallest of them, the one who'd shouted to him earlier, flicked his cigarette butt over the railings and looked at Katy.

"Do you know him?" he said. "Is he a perv?"

"Has he been following you?" said another.

David felt his umbrella being taken from him. A rattish lad in a baseball cap regarded the wooden handle and pressed the tip of his finger against the ferule.

All she had to do was say the word and they'd be onto him, and the thrill of knowing that seemed to run through Katy like electricity.

"Katy," said David. "You have to come with me."

She stared. She was going to deny him. But he didn't want to beg. He knew that if she were made to feel pity for him it would disgust her.

The chubby boy hung his arm around Katy's shoulder and said that he would kick David's balls in if she wanted. He kissed her on the ear, kissed her on the neck and after squirming under his touches Katy detached him with a quick blow to his stomach. He knelt on the wet boards trying to take a breath while his pals sent Katy and David on their way with threats and spit. David's umbrella clattered at their heels. A half-drunk can of lager skidded past them, spraying foam.

Katy didn't talk to David and walked ahead of him, hood up, hands in pockets. He hated having to know her. He wished that he could be like everyone else here who glanced at her once and forgot about her.

Unclouded now, the Tower rose to its full height and behind it the town unfolded street after street. He thought about telling Katy to lose herself for good, but by now Janet would be waiting on the prom with the car. She'd scold Katy, then hug her, then they'd take her to Mrs Yarrow's house and pretend that as long as they kept doing so life could carry on. But things had changed. She'd never run off like this before. A couple of years and she would be eighteen; five and she'd be twenty-one. They couldn't keep her confined to the house forever. Even if she didn't break a window or kick down a door, she would eventually outlive them and Mrs Yarrow.

He thought how bright the world would seem to her as she went out unlooked for and untreated for the first time. Having been forbidden so much for so long, and with no one to stop her, she'd gorge herself sick on sweets and men and bring to life all her persistent dreams of violence.

Still Water and Stars

By Carys Bray

It was the promise of singing that drew her to the car park in the gloaming of a Tuesday evening. The email said to wear warm clothes and bring a torch. She didn't usually go to the beach and she'd never been to that particular car park; she had to look it up on a map.

She found herself on the other side of town, at the better end of the beach; the part frequented by tourists – not in April, though. So, it was just them, the ones who'd got the email. The others stood around their cars, waiting, while she lingered in the warmth of hers. If things became uncomfortable or boring she would slip away home. This thought was accompanied by a picture of the wrong home and she sighed and reclined her seat a little, until she felt cradled by its back, and by the press of the driver's door against her shoulder.

Since moving house, she had discovered something animal in her; to sleep well, she needed the border of a wall or the cradle of a corner. The three of them, she, Dave and Toby, were sleeping on mattresses on the floors of their respective rooms. There was little point in loading the drawers or reassembling the wardrobes and beds because the upstairs floorboards cracked like fireworks and Dave said he would lift the carpet and screw the floorboards down – "When I get the chance, that's when." In the meantime, he was poring over work emails, trying to decide what the promise of 'self-sustaining services, operated on a cost-neutral basis' meant in relation to his contracted hours, and boxes of clothes, shoes, bedding and towels were stacked against the walls. She felt marooned; the mattress a boat on a sea of carpet. A streetlight pierced the previous owners' pale curtains. And she was being bitten by something in the night.

She reached for her ankle, where sock met skin, and, covering the hot bump of a bite with her index finger, scratched the surrounding flesh, hard as she could. The first itch was ecstasy. She knew she would regret the indulgence once she left the car to scale the dunes. Still, the bites would heal, eventually, and they weren't the worst of it.

Initially, she had been excited about the move. A smaller house would mean more manageable bills and reduced mortgage repayments; it would be a bulwark against further cuts in Dave's hours and lessen the annual summer anxiety as she waited to hear whether the college would renew her contract. Another recession was coming, Dave said. Best to be prepared.

The new house was closer to the station and the shops, meaning they could get rid of the car, if necessary. She had packed their belongings with a pragmatism that, in retrospect, seemed careless. Buy the worst house on the street – that's what she'd learned from watching property programmes. That's what they had done.

During the first night it rained and the pool of standing water on the porch's sagging, flat roof overflowed, causing the ceiling below to collapse. She had thought, for a moment, that the noise was safely outside, audible only because of the single-glazed windows. On investigation, she discovered shattered sections of plasterboard on the tiled porch floor and water pouring from a hole above. She called Dave who joined her on the stairs, belly and both hands balanced on the waistband of his underpants.

"Oh, God," he said. "At least the water's going straight out. See? Right under the door. There's nothing we can do about it now," and he shuffled back to bed.

Dave was right. She remained on the stairs watching, wondering why the door didn't seal properly and whether the move was going to be like one of Dave's diets; the reality of privation lost in the preparations: the buying of the right food, the calculations and measurements; all an inventive way to inflict misery, none of it a solution to anything.

In the days that followed, the house revealed itself. The back door was warped. To close it, she had to kick its bottom right corner. On its other side, in the stump of a severed tree, was a wasp nest with the arrival and departure schedule of an international airport. She wanted to call an exterminator, but Dave said he would get to it – 'When I get the chance, that's when.'

Living out of suitcases and boxes conjured a holiday feeling. Though the college was closed for Easter, her work emails continued to land. She glanced at the subject lines: 'Keeping in touch with emerging learning technologies,' 'Forging links with employers,' 'Developing an awareness of the policy landscape.' Each electronic interruption provoked the same reflexive response: she would deal with work once she returned home. But she *was* home. Greetings cards lined the mantelpiece, three bottles of congratulatory prosecco lay in the fridge and a pile of dirty laundry ripened and swelled beside the washing machine which would be plumbed in, eventually – when Dave got the chance, that's when.

"*I'm* going to live the kind of life where I don't need a holiday," Toby had declared, a couple of years ago, as he embarked on his A Levels.

That morning, she had asked both Dave and Toby, who had the night off work, whether they would like to accompany her to the beach. They refused.

"Fair enough," she responded. "I just thought I'd *do* something, you know? Have a go at living the kind of life where I don't need a holiday."

Toby frowned; there was no sign he remembered having said such a thing, and she suddenly missed his spiky over-confidence. During his year out he had travelled only as far as the promenade, where he'd found a part-time job trowelling chips into paper cones and polystyrene trays. She and Dave had been the first in their families to go to university. Trail-blazers, she had imagined, rather than exceptions to a rule. Toby had stopped talking about it. He said there would be more hours at the chippie in the summer, once the tourists arrived. Further discussion of his future only provided him with an excuse to highlight the precariousness of her job and Dave's increasing pessimism. She didn't know how to ask what was wrong without seeming to accuse him of something. Instead, she tried to bestow kindnesses. Toby smelled deep-fried; warm and salty, as if he had just stepped out of the sea. Before she left for the beach, she had plumbed in the washing machine with the help of an internet tutorial.

She glanced at her watch. Nine o'clock. She straightened her seat and opened the driver's door.

Outside, it was cool and breezy. The sky had dialled from dim to dark while she waited in the car. She followed the others to the edge of the car park where they huddled around a man in a ranger style hat and matching shorts. He introduced himself as Paul and took a register. Then they passed through a gate and into the dune system.

There were about twenty of them, every one middle-aged or older she reckoned, all decked out in sensible shoes and anoraks. The track was narrow, the sand solid, at first. They fell into line behind Paul, in pairs. Like many of the others, the man walking beside her was wearing a head-torch. She thought there were torches in one of the still packed kitchen boxes, but hadn't been able to find them, and had settled, instead, for charging her phone. But the light from his head-torch was enough to walk by.

The sand softened as they began to climb, cautiously, walking in the slippage of the people in front of them. They reached the top of a dune and she breathed deeply, her throat a whetstone to the cool breeze.

"These dunes stretch *all the way* to Liverpool," Paul said.

She was used to the northerly part of the beach, fringed by shops, amusements, Toby's chippie and, latterly, the addition of a food bank; a flat plane, protected by a sea wall; a place of looking *out* – or west – usually at bare sand, and a stripe of sea. The dunes were deeper than she had imagined, a range of peaks and troughs and winding paths. Standing at the brink of the hill, she looked *along* – or south – and felt her own smallness.

They slued down the dune's slipface. At the bottom Paul crouched and called for them to stop. He held out his hand, palm up.

"A natterjack," he said.

The toad was smaller than she'd expected. It looked ancient; so still that its skin seemed sculpted and bark-ish. Its back was bobbled by green lentil-like discs and dissected by a yellow stripe. She couldn't decide if its sheen was moisture or a trick of the torch light. Paul placed the toad on the ground. It didn't jump, but rather hurried away in a muscular combat-crawl.

Paul resumed walking and they followed.

"I'm Martin," said the man walking beside her.

"Hello," she replied.

"Have you been to one of these, before?" he asked.

"No," she said.

"That's a shame."

She didn't want to talk. She was there to listen – at that moment, to the breath of the other walkers; to the soft slide of their feet against the pitch of the dune; to the strokes and stabs of the capricious marram grass. Later, to the singing.

"You've not been to see the dragonflies?"

"No," she said.

"The wildflower walk?"

"No."

"Have you done the shipwreck tour?"

"Shipwreck?"

"Wrecks, actually. At Formby?"

"I didn't know there were any ship – "

"You should. It's a cracking evening."

As she walked sand spilled over the mesh tops of her trainers. She hadn't realised sand could be so cold.

"What about shrimping?" Martin tried.

"No."

"Now, the bat walk in Hesketh Park is a fun one. That's in the autumn, mind. Good for children, being so close to Halloween. Spooky."

Up ahead, perhaps believing the darkness bestowed anonymity, an old fellow burped; a wide-mouthed, trumpeting belch.

"Are you local?"

"Yes," she said, wondering whether Martin would move on to events everyone had heard of, and what he would think when he discovered that she hadn't been to any of them, either: the Air Show and the British Open Golf; the Musical Fireworks Championship and the Christmas pantomime. A few years ago, she won four Flower Show tickets in a raffle. Dave said it was a just a posh car boot sale and refused to go. Surprisingly, Toby and his friends requested the tickets; Ainsley Harriott was going to be there, and they had been watching videos of him on YouTube, marinating chicken breasts and saying, 'Give your meat a good old rub.' They wanted pictures with him. It would be a laugh, they said. On the day, she opened her winning envelope while the lads crowded the hall, whooping and yelping as they prodded each other. The envelope contained a slip of paper: *Call this number to order your complimentary tickets. Please allow at least two weeks for delivery.*

"Where do you live, then?" Martin asked as they paused at the brink of another dune.

She thought of the old house. Occasionally, having checked the forecast, she would hang out the washing just before bedtime. There was a sycamore tree in the garden that Toby had brought home on his last day at nursery; a stick wrapped in a soggy cardboard roll. It had come with a poem, something mawkish with a line about tiny hands and another about eventual goodbyes. By the time Toby had finished his first year at school, the stick had grown into a tree. On those evenings when she hung the washing out, she would watch Toby's tree for a moment, tall and skinny, its leaves like pennies in the pale yellow of a streetlight on the road behind the house. It was a small view, framed on each side by the garden hedge. There, at the top of the dune, she absorbed the bare beauty of the scene; the hemisphere of the sky, the waning moon sitting among the stars like a lonely speckled egg, and it occurred to her that the new people could cut Toby's tree down if they felt like it.

"Where do you live?" Martin asked, again.

"Sorry, I was thinking –" she paused. "I just moved."

"Ah-ha," Martin replied, as if he had finally got to the bottom of things. "Where from?"

"Oh, from here," she said. "I've always lived here."

She discovered the cassette in a box that had moved, unopened, to each of their rented flats and, eventually, to the old house, where it had sat in the dusty warmth of the loft for more than a decade. It was a mixtape, made by an old friend: recordings of the choir to which they had belonged and excerpts of concertos and choral pieces they had studied in A Level music lessons. She stuffed it in her hoodie pocket and threw the rest of the box's contents – English exercise books, old essays and manuscript paper – in the bin. The cassette was still in her pocket when she unpacked Dave's old ghetto blaster and placed it on the kitchen worktop in the new house. She hadn't played a cassette for years and she wondered whether the tape might break or noodle out of the roller openings. It worked, though, and her old school choir provided the soundtrack to their first days in the new house. She wiped out cupboards and rubbed almond floor cleaner into the sticky laminate as her eighteen-year-old self sang in the background. At first, she only listened. Eventually, she joined in, her voice thin and stale.

"This is me," she began, when Toby appeared, pyjamaed and yawning. "Me and my friends, when I was –"

"I *know*," he replied. "You've already told me."

She rubbed the floor hard, head down. Eventually, he finished his coffee, and shambled out of the kitchen. She put the cloth in the sink and made herself a drink. The unread free newspaper sat on the top of the recycling box and she flicked it open.

'Birkdale Nightingales' – that's how natterjacks were described in the article advertising the walk in the dunes. The excursion reminded her of the kinds of trips they had taken when Toby was smaller and they'd been able to afford proper holidays: a boat tour around Loch Ness, dolphin watching in West Wales, seal spotting in Norfolk. Places were always interesting when she was on holiday. There was a different way of seeing, an expectation of being pleased and of finding beauty, something she had hoped Toby would discover in the course of his year out. It was harder to appreciate a place when you moved around it every day; you stopped watching and listening, parts became invisible. She had driven past the dunes but never set foot in them. And all this time, they had been filled with beautiful music. It seemed remarkable that she hadn't known, and imperative that she hear the Birkdale Nightingales for herself.

Eventually, they reached a dip in the dunes and Paul stopped. The valley sloped further and she could see the edge of a pool. They were sheltered from the breeze there, and it was quiet.

"We're standing in a slack," he said.

They gathered round him in a circle, listening, headtorches like candle flames.

"A slack is damp hollow that floods in winter. You've got forty percent of the country's dune slacks right here, on this stretch of coast. During winter, the natterjacks hibernate in deep burrows. In spring, when the weather improves, they emerge and, hopefully, discover a pond to breed in. They're mostly nocturnal. And, as you know, the males sing to attract a mate. Later in the year, the ponds evaporate, and the slacks become a habitat for wildflowers. In winter, the floods. In summer, the flowers."

She bent to scratch her ankle while Paul talked about the historic loss of almost eighty percent of natterjack breeding sites, the subsequent protection of both toad and habitat, and the recent increase in population thanks to careful management and conservation.

"Right, lights off, everyone," he said.

She straightened as the torches went out. In the instant before her eyes adjusted, the dark was bottomless.

"The natterjacks are the loudest amphibian in Europe," he spoke in a whisper, now. "Let's see if they'll sing for us, tonight."

This was it. The moment she would wrap up and take back with her. A transcendent moment; one she might re-live at night when her life ticked loudly – there would be something soothing in the knowledge that, a couple of miles away, at the edge of everything, there was singing.

She listened and heard the hush of the others. Their breath. Someone's sleeves brushed the puff of their jacket.

"*There*," Paul whispered. "Listen!"

It was a lonely sound, at first. A solitary, grinding croak. It sounded like a guiro; like a stick rubbing along the notches of a wooden cylinder. She supposed it was a sort of warm-up. But then the lone performer was joined by other, similarly raucous voices. She felt the beginnings of a laugh in her throat and swallowed it down. The singing was horrid.

The noise sawed back and forth, back and forth, more shout than song; a corrugated bark that reminded her of something annoying about the old house: an over-sensitive burglar alarm on a neighbouring street that had screamed to life at least once a week. The natterjacks' singing was lower than the alarm,

119

though, and less invasive. It had a warmer blare, she decided: drilling, penetrative and, she conceded, eventually, not entirely unpleasant.

As time passed, it began to feel familiar; an old music that bridged the gap between the still water and the stars. And, as much as it was a call to the females, it was also, she imagined, an anthem to the elements; to the wind that had scoured the sand to form the slack and the rain that had landed there – perhaps some of the same rain had burst through her porch ceiling. There was a hypnotic quality to the music. She closed her eyes and listened.

On the way back, they fell back into line behind Paul. Once they left the slack, it was quiet, the only sounds the breeze and their own noises as they climbed and descended. Martin walked beside her, subdued, emptied of questions. She recalled Paul's earlier comment: *In winter, the floods. In summer, the flowers.*

"You mentioned a wildflower walk," she said.

"I did," Martin agreed.

"Sounds interesting," she offered.

"It's at the rifle range, at Altcar. In June. I don't suppose you've been, before?"

"No."

"You'll need to email ahead, same as today."

"Right."

"When you get to Altcar, you check in at the Guard House. Then you cross the pontoon bridge over the River Alt and follow the road round. Ignore the first, small car park and keep going until you get to the bigger one, by the meadows. That's where we'll be waiting. They'll tell you all that when you book your place."

"Okay," she said.

"There's orchids, and cowslips, and Ragged Robin. Primroses. Lady's Bedstraw. It's beautiful."

Cold sand poured into the backs of her trainers as she took skidding steps down the slipface of the dune.

"And," Martin added, as they reached the bottom, "you'll need to make sure you bring your passport. The site's run by the Reserve Forces," he added by way of explanation. "They can't be too careful."

But she wasn't listening. She was wondering where she had put the passports. Perhaps in one of the bedroom boxes. They would be unpacked by the summer – Dave would surely have the floorboards done by then. She blew her cold hands and stuffed them into her coat pockets. It would be like going on holiday.

CONTRIBUTORS

LOUISE AYRE was born in Salford in 1986 and grew up in West Cumbria. Her writing often explores mental health issues and their wide-reaching impact. She is currently working on her debut novel *When We Were Gods* and does much of her writing during her train commute. She lives in Surrey with her partner, their badly-behaved cat, two guinea pigs and a leaning tower of books. When not writing, her time is spent trying to complete the Rory Gilmore Reading Challenge or watching funny cat videos.

CARYS BRAY is the author of two novels and a short story collection. Her first novel *A Song for Issy Bradley* was shortlisted for the Costa First Novel Award and won the Authors' Club Best First Novel Award. She has written for BBC radio and her fiction has appeared in a variety of magazines and anthologies. Carys lives in Southport. She is working on a third novel.

BETHAN ELLIS was born in Southend-on-Sea. She studied English at Cambridge, and Writing at Warwick University. She was part of the founding team at grassroots publisher And Other Stories, and is a member of PICA, an artist-led studio based in York, where she now lives. She is studying for a PhD in Literary Practice at Warwick, and her current project is a novel set on the margins of the Thames Estuary.

ANDREW MICHAEL HURLEY is the author of two short story collections, *Cages* and *The Unusual Death of Julie Christie*. His first novel, *The Loney*, was originally published in 2014 by

Tartarus Press and then John Murray a year later, after which it won the 2015 Costa 'First Novel' award and the 2016 British Book Industry awards for 'Debut Novel' and 'Book of the Year.' His second novel, *Devil's Day*, was published in October 2017. The author lives in Lancashire with his family and teaches Creative Writing at Manchester Metropolitan University's Writing School.

PETE KALU's short story, 'Getting Home' can be found in the Peepal Tree short story collection, *Closure* (Peepal Tree 2015). His science fiction short story, 'Doppelganger' can be found in the *Manchester Review* July 2017. His science fiction novel *Black Star Rising* (X Press) will be republished in 2018 by Venture Press. 'The Keeper of Books' draws from three sources: the history, *A Jamaican Plantation* by Michael Craton and James Walvin; Jonathan Swift's *A Tale of a Tub*; and Joseph Senhouse's *Memoirs*, a document held at Cumbria Record Office (Whitehaven).

PAUL KINGSNORTH is the author of two novels: *The Wake*, which was long listed for the 2014 Man Booker Prize, and *Beast*. He has also published three books of non-fiction. His most recent book is his second poetry collection, *Songs From The Blue River*, published by Salmon in 2018. He is co-founder of the Dark Mountain Project, an international collective of writers and artists. He lives in Ireland.

KIRSTY LOGAN is the author of short story collection *The Rental Heart and Other Fairytales*, awarded the Polari First Book Prize and the Saboteur Award for Best Short Story Collection, and debut novel *The Gracekeepers*, awarded a Lambda Literary Award. Her most recent book, *A Portable Shelter*, is a collection of linked short stories inspired by Scottish folktales and was published in a limited edition with custom woodblock illustrations. Her next novel, *The Gloaming*, is out in May 2018. She is currently working on a collection of short horror stories, a TV pilot script, and a musical collaboration project.

ANITA SETHI was born and bred in Manchester, UK, and spent many childhood holidays in Blackpool. Her short stories and essays have been published in anthologies including the *Seasons* nature writing anthology, *Roads Ahead*, *Solstice Shorts*, and *From There to Here* and she has been an International Writer in Residence at the Emerging Writers Festival in Melbourne, Australia. She has written for publications including *The Guardian* and *Observer*, *The Sunday Times*, *Telegraph*, *Times Literary Supplement*, *Granta* and *New Statesman*, and appeared on BBC radio.

MELISSA WAN is from Manchester by way of Hong Kong. She began writing for the stage, and went on to study sociology and urban theory. As a result, she fell in love with Walter Benjamin's city snapshots, which first inspired her to write prose. Her current influences include Grace Paley, Miranda July and Rosie Garland. 'The Husband and the Wife Go to the Seaside' is her first published story.

LUCY WILKINSON YATES was born in Preston in 1986. She is a recent graduate of the Centre For New Writing MA programme at Manchester University. Her fiction has previously been published in *The Manchester Anthology 2017*, *Barcelona Stories* and *The Gift Issue* (New Niu Press, Barcelona), and shortlisted for the VIII Certamen Internacional de Microrrelatos de San Fermin.